Summer of '52

Judith Rice

Summer of '52

Summer of '52 is a work of fiction.
All characters, places, conversations, and stories are purely products
of the author's imagination. Any resemblance to a place or person,
living or dead, is purely coincidental.

ISBN 978-0-692-18958-0

Cover photographs provided by the Lyda Hill Texas Collection of
Photographs in Carol M. Highsmith's America Project, Library of
Congress, Prints and Photographs Division.

Cover Design by Agustina Giannico

SailAway

For my family, near and far,
past and present,
with eternal love and gratitude.

For Jane —
Enjoy this "Summer"
read !
All the best —
Judy

Everything is different,
yet nothing ever changes.

Loosely translated from an epigram by Jean-Baptiste
Alphonse Karr, published in "Les Guêpes" in 1849:
"plus ça change, plus c'est la même chose"

Table of Contents

Coming Home   9

Ole Buttermilk Sky   33

The Vase   57

Why Me, Lord?   67

Cheers!   83

Nobody's Child   103

Jailbait   131

Refuge from the Storm   151

When the Bow Breaks   171

Shame!   191

A Good Heart   215

Acknowledgements   253

About the Author   255

Coming Home

Dottie pushes each of the wooden legs of her folding chair into the sandy slope to level it so when she sits, it won't pitch her forward into the gravel pit. She would rather be most anywhere else, but today, Memorial Day, she'll go fishing with Vern, if only to keep him out of the tavern, keep him from embarrassing her and Rosie in front of their friends at the church. She mops the bead of sweat from her upper lip with her tongue and tugs on the arms of the chair to make sure it's secure. She adjusts her hat, eyes the water. It's deep, dangerously deep, right to the very edge. *Over my head*, she thinks. *Can't even see the bottom. If I fall in, I die. Then what would happen to Rosie?*

She sees Vern watching her, sees him smirk. He knows she's afraid of the water. He moves closer and says, "You know, if you fall in, you'll float 'cause you got plenty of padding." He gives her a sharp slap on her backside, then grabs her shoulders and pretends to push her toward the water. He laughs. She shakes free, heart racing, fighting an urge to scream, fighting so as to not give him the satisfaction. *Why does he think this is funny?* She sits down in her chair, stares at the water, waits for him to bait her hook.

She remembers the panic like it was yesterday. She is five years old, the youngest of six kids and they are all at their favorite lake cottage for summer vacation. Little Dottie is sitting close to the water's edge, playing with her shovel and bucket, listening to her dad and brothers splash around at the far end of the dock.

Her dad calls out to her, "Hey Dottie! Come 'ere! Somethin' I gotta show ya!"

She leaves her bucket on the beach and runs down to the end of the dock to see what it is.

Then her dad yells, "Jump! Come on, Dottie! Jump in! Don't be a scaredy-cat!" He motions her to come to him and promises, "It's not over your head here! Jump! I got 'cha." Trusting him, she jumps off the end of the dock.

She knows instantly that she can't touch bottom. She can't reach him, can't touch the dock. She struggles to the surface, gasping for air, choking, arms flailing, bobbing up and down trying to reach him. She can see him—he's laughing and reaching out to her. She can't get to him. She goes under again.

Finally, he grabs her and flings her up on the dock, berating her for being afraid, then daring her to jump again. "I wasn't gonna drown ya! This is how I learn ya to swim."

She sobs and coughs, runs toward the safety of the cottage. She never did learn to swim.

Dottie leans back in her chair at the edge of the water, each hand gripping the cane fishing pole, watching and waiting for the tip of the bobber to disappear under the water. She fears that a fish on the line could catch her off guard and drag her straight out into the water. *That'd be the end of me!* Seconds later, the bobber does go under and she feels the tug on the pole. "Oh, oh! Vern! Help! I have a fish!"

The unseen fish darts from side to side, pulling the bobber and the line back and forth with it, then it heads out toward the middle of the water, which scares her half to death. She clutches the pole, and just as Vern yells, "Pull it in!" she pulls the pole straight up and back over her head. The fish on the end of the line breaks the water and sails right toward her face! Seeing this, she screams, "Noooooo!" and instantly feels the sharpness of the back fin on her cheek.

In a frenzy, she drops the pole and tries to get out of her chair. Vern, seeing this, yells, "Don't lose the pole and don't fall in!" Dottie, terrified, backs into her seat while the fish, a big whiskered catfish, flops back and forth in the sand next to her. Vern calmly sets his pole aside, takes the fish off her hook, and, after pretending to throw it to her, throws it in the bucket next to her chair.

Under her breath, she asks, "Why do you think that's funny?"

"It's a keeper," he says, then baits her hook with another big night crawler, casts it back into the water and hands her the pole. This goes on all morning. She always catches more fish than he does. After she settles in, Dottie uses this time to think about things—her life here in Springdale, how different it is than she thought it would be those many years ago.

They hadn't known it when they left their childhood home in the Ozarks a dozen years back, but the war was just around the corner. Even before the war, the plant in Springdale was hiring. Like many others from their corner of the world, they packed up their belongings and moved north to Springdale. For Dottie, it meant leaving her extended family and childhood friends behind, but for Vern, it meant being able to support his family. There were no prospects of finding a decent job in his home town.

Now Springdale is home, but it hasn't always felt that way. In fact, it could be mighty lonely here for newcomers, especially in those first years. She'd had no real friends to celebrate with in good times, and worse, no one to lean on in bad times.

After the war broke out, all the men who were not too old or infirm joined up. Vern tried, but they wouldn't take him, he said, because he was deaf in one ear. The Springdale plant that had hired Vern was one of many ordered by the nation's War Production Board to retool for making weapons, machinery and munitions, and anyone who could work was needed to man their production lines. All the women like Dottie who were fit and didn't have small children at home piled on and worked the assembly lines right alongside the older and disabled men for the duration of the war. The war effort had bonded Dottie and Vern to one another and to their new community—it seemed to have given them purpose.

Dottie quit the plant just before the end of the war, hoping to start a family, and it was then that she'd had her third and most devastating miscarriage. It was a boy, the doctor said, a son. She'd carried him almost five months, well after she had felt life. She had been overjoyed to get beyond the three-month mark, past the time she'd lost the other two. She was starting to show, but perhaps because she is heavyset, no one seemed to notice—no one asked if she was expecting. She had insisted they keep her condition secret for fear of inviting another miscarriage, but she couldn't resist buying a few baby things for her layette at the church bazaar—a yellow (for a girl or a boy) baby blanket with kittens embroidered on it, a darling stuffed teddy bear, diapers and pins, all tucked away in her cedar chest. She didn't even tell Vern.

When she lost that baby too, just days later, they were both heartbroken. She blamed herself for being too happy, for tempting fate. She had told no one, not even her family back home. *What would be the use of telling them? They are so far away—what could they do?*

Dottie took to her bed for the longest time, and Vern took to the bottle. He continued to work the second shift at the plant and framed houses in the mornings, weather permitting. Every Saturday he would drop his entire carpenter's paycheck at Staley's Tavern, then come home drunk. Dottie would sometimes go fishing with him on Saturday mornings, thinking that if she went with him, it would keep him out of the tavern. She hated the gravel pit, but even more, hated the smell of beer and the meanness it brought out in Vern. She railed at him and threatened to leave him, but it made no difference. Besides, where could she go?

Dottie finally pulled herself together, made a few friends through the Women's Circle at the Methodist Church, and, believing she would be childless all of her life, went to work behind the butcher counter at Goodman's Market. Vern was rarely home during the week except for dinner before he went to work at the plant. On Sundays, he stayed in bed recovering from his Saturday binges. He never would go to church with her.

Several years after the war ended, Dottie heard through her church that the children's home downtown was closing and placing eight children into foster homes. Vern promised her on their Bible that if they could get a child, he'd quit drinking. He'd be a good father. She challenged him, "Quit now." And he did. For a while.

They filled out the application for a child, then waited for word from the agency through the Spring. Finally, the social worker, Mrs. Goble, called Dottie and told her they had an eight-year-old girl to place right after school was out. "Most people want babies or toddlers, but this is a nice older child who needs a home," she went on, "plus we have no babies or toddlers at the moment. What do you think?"

It took no time at all for Dottie to answer, "Yes, of course! This is wonderful news! What's her name? And when can we meet her?"

"Rosweeta is her given name, but she likes to be called Rosie. And you can come to meet her next weekend, on Saturday morning."

With her hand over the mouthpiece, Dottie, almost out of breath, said, "Vern! It's the adoption people. They have an eight-year-old girl for us named Rosie! Oh my, oh my, Vern—a child!" Dottie couldn't stop smiling.

"And what does the mister think?" Mrs. Goble asked.

"Vern says, 'why yes, he always hoped for a girl.'"

"Very well, then. I'll see you at the home on Saturday morning."

Come Saturday, Dottie and Vern, dressed in their Sunday best, went to the county home to meet the girl. Mrs. Goble ushered them into the room where the children sat on the floor listening to a story. She pointed out Rosie and said they could watch the children while she gets her paperwork in order. Dottie whispered to Vern, "Rosie seems older than most of the others. And look, Vern, she's the only child there wearing glasses. She must be real smart!"

They sat to the side, Dottie whispering comments to Vern, both watching Rosie talk to the little kids. "Look Vern. They seem to really like her."

When Mrs. Goble came back, she told them Rosie could visit them next weekend, but since the child didn't yet know that she was to be placed, she wouldn't introduce them today.

Dottie, tickled pink, talked about nothing else to Vern for hours on end. They talked about her as though she were already theirs, then Dottie remembered their disappointments with the babies they'd lost, and clammed up.

Mrs. Goble had told them that the girl had had a chaotic childhood, often farmed out to her mother's friends, or friends of friends, then after those arrangements fell apart, she lived in two other orphanages, and finally, in the county home where she was now. Still, Dottie was sure, if they were given half a chance, they could give Rosie a loving home.

Rosie's weekend visit put Dottie and Vern on cloud nine. Of course, they didn't tell her that they hoped she was soon to be placed with them, but they wished they could just keep her. She was such a darling girl—a perfect fit for them! After the weekend, Dottie had gone out and bought a matching set—hairbrush, mirror and comb—and a new quilt for the bed. She bought several pieces of fabric and some patterns to make her some summer clothes, and started sewing right away. The very next week, Mrs. Goble called and told them everything was in order, that she had recommended they be approved as prospective parents. As soon as the judge gave his approval, she told Dottie, Rosie would come to live with them. After one year, if all went well, the court would make the adoption final.

Dottie will never forget the day Rosie came to stay! She was clutching a flowery card that said "Happy Mother's Day." Dottie saw the card, and even though Mother's Day had passed, she was touched that this little girl was bringing her a Mother's Day card. Already! When Mrs. Goble suggested to Rosie that she give the card to Dottie, Rosie, shaking her head no, whispered something to Mrs. Goble who then whispered back, "*She* is your mother now." After an awkward moment, Rosie, refusing to make eye contact with Dottie, handed her the card. Dottie thought to embrace her, but Rosie slipped just out of her reach. Only then did Dottie realize that Rosie didn't know she would never see her mother again. It just about broke Dottie's heart.

Despite the rocky start, Dottie remembers with great fondness that first summer with Rosie. She loves to tell the story of when they became a family.

"It was a dream come true for me, Rosie. And Daddy? Right before he'd go to the plant, he would go out back and pick a peony for you. He'd bring it into the kitchen and I'd put it in a jar with water for you. He'd never done that before, even for me. And on Saturdays, he would take us for a ride in the truck. Remember when we went to the street fair?

"The whole community, especially the Goodman clan, they were so kind when I told them we were going to be parents. The church women, too. Right before we got you, they all acted like I was going to have a baby, giving me a shower and all, even though you weren't a baby. We were a real family back then!"

Rosie always listens, but she doesn't tell her story. Dottie never pries.

Today, she and Rosie will celebrate Memorial Day with the Goodmans, and Rosie will tend to their youngest kids. Dottie loves to watch them with Rosie—all those kids, stair-steps, from the baby to the twelve-year-old—towheads, every one of them. Rosie babysits regularly when Mrs. Goodman goes to choir practice at the church—she's part of their family too. No money ever changes hands.

Sitting there, staring into the deep water, Dottie reflects on the year just past—*a difficult one for me and for Goodman's Market.*

Last February, she took a bad fall on the ice just outside the shop. By the time Mr. Goodman got her home, the neighbors said she didn't know where she was or even maybe who she was. They had to intercept Rosie on her way home from school, because they weren't at all sure Dottie would know her. The doctor allowed that she had managed to get a pretty bad concussion, so he prescribed bed rest for about four weeks all together. Goodman had to find someone to pinch hit for her, but he kept right on paying her as though she were still working.

"She's family," Goodman said. "You don't wash your hands of family because they get a bump on the noggin, do you? We all help each other out," he said, then he winked at Dottie, handed her a paycheck, and that was that.

Then, right after Dottie went back to work from her concussion, Vern had a wreck and had to go to the hospital.

He was out of work for two weeks, then had to ride to work with Jon down the street while the car was being fixed. She's still relieved it wasn't worse than it was, because they don't have any savings at all. Mr. Goodman never mentioned anything about the wreck, even though everyone in town knows Vern was darn sure drunk when it happened.

He started drinking again even before the one-year trial period for Rosie's adoption was up. Throughout that year, he had quit and started again too many times to count. Dottie was deathly afraid someone, even Rosie herself, would tell the adoption agency about him drinking and they'd take Rosie back. He kept saying he'd quit, but he never did.

Now, about the only time Rosie sees Vern is on Saturdays, when he comes home drunk. She hides in her room when he comes home because, as she says, he scares her when he's drunk. She still remembers that one Saturday last year, he came home angry and smashed a two-layer cake that Dottie had made with his hand, then threw the mess across the kitchen floor. Dottie cried, and Rosie locked herself into her bedroom for the rest of the day.

More often than not these days, Rosie is at the Goodmans' home on Saturday evenings helping Mrs. Goodman with the children. And she'll often just spend the night so she can help get everyone ready for church in the morning. Dottie doesn't blame Rosie for not wanting to be in the house with Vern, but she misses her terribly. Sometimes, when Rosie is at the Goodmans, Dottie cries herself to sleep.

As if these troubles aren't bad enough, Dottie sees first-hand the difficulty the Goodmans have trying to keep up with the brand-new Kroger store. It just moved in a few blocks away. Goodman's is a small grocery store, mostly a butcher shop, but he's always stocked pretty much whatever else folks need. Most of the women still shop at Goodman's, and they tell Dottie it's because of her and the Goodman family—it's about trust. Plus, the meat is better, they say. And they say they don't want to see Goodman's close down like the Stark Eatery did after the Howard Johnson's opened up. But some folks have told Dottie they do wish he would start giving Green Stamps, like Kroger does. In fact, she saw that her friend Stella had a pile of Green Stamp books on her kitchen counter, one almost full. She didn't say anything, but it worries her.

Vern yells, "Dottie," and she shakes off her reverie, reluctantly. "We've caught our limit. Let's go on home." Dottie figures he's itching to get back so he can go to

Staley's, which he does on any special occasion. All he ever wants to do when he isn't working is hang at the tavern with his drinking buddies. Then come home drunk as a skunk. Dottie had heard that he buys rounds of beer for all of the men in the bar—drunks, all of them. Of course, they love to see him come in.

He takes the pole from her hands and loads the truck with all the gear. Dottie climbs in the front seat and props her arm on the open window. On their way home, she notices folks already along the parade route, and others readying their groups for the march to the cemetery. When they get home, Vern cleans the fish, then tells Dottie he has some people to see about carpenter work and leaves in his truck. She knows what that means.

She changes her clothes, donning the new dress she'd made for just this occasion and bustles to the designated meeting place for the parade participants. Rosie will meet her here with whichever Goodman kids are coming to the parade, so she waits and chats with her friends about the weather and the beautiful day ahead.

As she surveys the gathering crowd, she spots Louise, who works at Springdale Five & Dime. Louise had helped her pick out the pattern and material for the new dress she's wearing today—red and white striped polished cotton with blue bias tape for pocket trim. Dottie had felt her face flush when Louise advised her that plump women should wear only vertical stripes, "*never, never* horizontal, as the horizontals call attention to the waistline." Louise had also offered to help her pin and fit the dress, so, as she said, "it would look store-bought rather than homemade." S*nazzy* was the word that had come to mind when Dottie looked in the mirror this morning. The red, white, and blue—perfect for this occasion. Still, she wished Louise hadn't called attention to her figure.

Now feeling a bit self-conscious, she corrects her posture, smooths her dress over her waistline, and glances around anxiously. She pulls a crisp white handkerchief from her pocket, dabs at her forehead. She catches Louise's eye, smiles and nods slightly while holding her skirt to the side as in a curtsy.

She listens to the chair of the parade committee search for the various groups: "Twirlers? Cheerleaders? You need to get over here too. And Phillip?"

Phillip, the high school drum major, sashays up to Dottie.

"You look fabulous, Phillip!"

"So do you, Miss Dottie. I love your red, white and blue outfit!"

She eyes his drum major hat with gold braids, a plume and tassels. "And I love your hat!" Phillip smiles and nods as if bowing, then turns to go to the parade staging area.

Dottie sees Rosie heading toward her with two of the Goodman boys, and they all watch as Phillip steps out into the street to take his place just behind the Honor Guard and in front of the twirlers. He is in high gear, baton in hand, head thrown back in a haughty stance, and they talk about how the gold accents on his uniform sparkle in the sunlight. He turns to watch the parade assembling behind him.

The twirlers are now a safe distance behind Phillip, throwing and catching their batons, twirling continuously. The cheerleaders with their pom-poms are individually rehearsing their moves, and Lena, the captain of the squad, is out in front. She hands off her pom-poms to the coach, adjusts her costume, shakes her head and fiddles with her hair, then performs a cartwheel and a flip, all in the snap of a finger, previewing what's in store for the crowd along the parade route. Phillip applauds while Rosie and Dottie nod in approval.

Dottie says to Rosie, "She makes it look so easy, doesn't she?" Rosie, deep in thought, nods.

As the groups take their places, something catches Dottie's eye and she threads her way through the marchers, over to the small group of women, most dressed in black.

They are Springdale's Gold Star Mothers. Dottie greets them, touching softly, gently hugging each of them. She knows many of these women, some better than others. Every one of them has lost a son to war, most in WWII, though her neighbor Ursula, who she doesn't see here, lost her boy, Norman, in Korea just a year ago. *Her son hadn't even been buried by Memorial Day last year.*

She asks the group, "Has anyone spoken with Ursula today?"

One of the women says, "Yes. She said she won't walk in the parade this year."

Dottie nods and, for a moment, stands motionless. Everyone in town feels for Norman's family. Everyone talked about him last year, including the minister at the service. They all said he was such a nice kid. And he was.

Just the kind of son I thought we might have, the one we lost before he was even born. So long ago. She feels the sting of her tears, then jerks her head up and walks back to Rosie.

She takes a moment to look back on the scene of the Gold Star Mothers, and is relieved to see her pastor, Reverend J.B., has joined them. She admires him so much. Everyone does. He always has a kind word for even those who don't go to his church.

Dottie steps up onto the bandstand to survey the town's people alongside the road, some in lawn chairs, some standing, kids running out into the road and being called back by anxious parents—all waiting in the cool breeze for the parade to pass by. And just as in the years past, she knows most will fall in behind the parade and walk to the cemetery.

This town always turns out for its fallen.

The parade grand marshal bellows, "Sheriff Tyler— We're ready!"

He smiles, waves, then flips the siren switch on and off a few times, making a boop-boop sound, as he drives in slow motion, zigzagging back and forth, clearing the way, signaling the beginning of the parade.

The players have their instruments at the ready, the twirlers have stilled their batons and the cheerleaders are standing at parade attention. Those who can see Phillip are watching him, waiting for their cue.

Dottie hears the parade marshal speak to Phillip, "Let's do it, son!"

Phillip gives the drummers a downbeat and they begin their slow cadence. The four men carrying flags, drummers flanking them, step out and proceed down Main Street toward the cemetery. Unexpectedly, she feels chills up and down her back at the sounds of the solemn march.

Now Phillip stands tall, his baton high in the air. All eyes are on him. He faces the band, gives the downbeat, and they play, by heart, "Hail to Old Westside High," to the tune of "Anchors Aweigh." Phillip marches backward, keeping the tempo by jabbing the air with his baton. At the end of the second phrase, he whirls around and marches forward, never missing a beat.

Dottie, Rosie by her side, is smiling, "You know, Rosie, he's different than all the other boys. Phillip, I mean. He's such a showman and always respectful! I really like him."

Rosie smiles and nods.

Dottie and Rosie and the Goodman boys ride with the deputy, who is a friend of Mr. Goodman, and is bringing up the rear of the parade. Dottie is relieved that Vern isn't on the parade route—so far, that is. Everyone who's standing along the route is waving a flag and cheering. Just as she expected.

At the cemetery, folks gather around the podium. The Gold Star families have special seating up front where Jon, Norman's father, is sitting. Phillip, the twirlers, Lena, and the cheerleaders all stand quietly to the side of the band while the invocation is given. The grand marshal reads the list of Springdale's fallen soldiers and sailors, where and when they died. The last name on the list is Norman, Ursula and Jon's son, Lena's brother, who died last May in Korea onboard his ship. It had been years since the last son was lost, but of course, they were all being remembered today. As several mothers had said to Dottie, the pain never really goes away.

All is quiet for a few moments, then the band plays "America the Beautiful" in honor of the last fallen soldier. Some people join in singing the chorus. Dottie is looking around at the crowd when she sees Ursula walk through the cemetery gate. She's holding a bouquet of zinnias with one lanky stalk of larkspur jutting out from the center, the deep blue flowers standing proud above the rainbow of zinnias. She walks across the grass toward the mothers, and when she reaches them, they surround her in a protective cocoon. Phillip holds his hand out to Lena. She moves to his side, closes her eyes, and rests her head on his shoulder. There is not a dry eye in the crowd. Everyone in this small town knew Norman.

Dottie feels a wave of patriotism mixed with sorrow. She had been heartbroken when Ursula received the devastating news. They all had. Today, she stays close to her Rosie, holding hands while the band plays, and she keeps an eye on Ursula. *It's been a tough year for them.*

The band leader picks up his bugle and plays "Taps." No one moves except Ursula. She walks, unaccompanied, to her son's grave and places the bouquet she's carrying on his gravestone. They had refused burial at Arlington— Ursula wanted him close by.

Touched by her gesture of love and grief, Dottie, Phillip, Lena, and Jon move quietly to join Ursula. They hug and walk back to join the other families who have already decorated their sons' graves.

This ceremony was necessarily somber, but soon, everyone will gather at the park for a huge potluck and ice cream social put on by the Women's Circle of the Methodist Church and the cookie sale put on by the Women's Guild at St. Mary's. There'll be square dancing, pony rides for the little kids, raffles to buy homemade pies and cakes. The Wabash Boys, the high school group who plays popular songs for dancing, will be on the bandstand until nightfall.

One by one, the families depart the cemetery, some stopping to chat to bridge the gap between this solemn ceremony and the festivities ahead. Many of the ladies stop to talk about what a great job the town's people did, especially the parade committee. Thankfully, it all went well. As the crowd thins, Dottie makes her way to Phillip to tell him how perfect he was in the parade, and what a good person he is to help Lena and Ursula.

Even though she misses the beautiful Ozark woods of her childhood, it is at moments like this that Dottie reflects on Springdale—*this unremarkable place without a hill or a stream, this place studded with corn fields, lilacs and colorful maples, this place where people help each other— this is my home.* And it is home because she and Rosie have become part of the community. They're part of these people, all caring for each other. All family.

She tries to give her daughter a big hug, but Rosie slips just out of her grasp. Dottie believes that one day she will feel safe enough to allow a hug. For now, Dottie takes her hand and teases, "You know what, Rosie? You're my favorite kid!"

"I'm your only kid, Mom."

"Of course, you're right. And I wouldn't have it any other way! C'mon. Let's go to the park and have some ice cream."

Ole Buttermilk Sky

Rosie idolizes Lena. Not just because she is sixteen (Rosie's thirteen, going on fourteen), nor because Lena has made the cheerleading squad, though both are good enough reasons. Her true fascination with Lena is that she taps. On stage! In fact, she takes tap, acrobatics and modern dance, all from Mr. Richard, who is, as Lena's mother always says, "the only real dance teacher in town."

Rosie pleads for tap lessons, but her mother argues, "It's just not practical. What can you do with that when you grow up? Better you learn to sew or iron, or ride your bike on over to the church and practice the piano. And when you can play like Liberace, then you can take tap."

It isn't that Rosie doesn't like taking piano lessons. She does. But can't her mom understand? Playing the piano is nothing like tap dancing!

The two girls' fathers both work the second shift at the plant. And since Lena's house is the only one in their neighborhood with a TV, her mom, Miss Ursula, will call Rosie's mom, "TV's coming in good tonight. So-and-so is on at 7:00. Why don't you and Rosie come on over?"

Invariably, as the show starts, the picture begins to fade to snow and all they can hear is static. Miss Ursula, Lena's mom, always tries to fix it by turning the aerial on the roof from a dial on top of the TV set. Sometimes it fixes the picture, but usually not. When that happens, Miss Ursula makes popcorn, and the mothers play canasta at the kitchen table, filling the house with sounds of whispering followed by boisterous laughter intermingled with the smell of fresh popcorn and the crisp sound of cards being shuffled.

On these evenings, Lena is stuck with Rosie. Her mother tells her, "It's not polite to make Rosie sit in the living room all by herself. Why don't you two girls go on in your room and play Parcheesi?"

They usually do go into Lena's room, but they never play Parcheesi. In fact, Lena usually ignores Rosie.

Lena's bedroom furniture is all blonde—two twin beds and between them, a dresser with a mirror. The whole room smells of Evening in Paris, the perfume that sits on the dresser alongside her enormous piggy bank with her name in gold letters on both sides. A single sleeping pink flamingo, one leg tucked up under its body, beak resting on its back, spans the length of each of the white chenille bedspreads—souvenirs from their Florida vacation—and the pink rug between the beds is fluffy, as though no one ever steps on it.

Lena perches on one flamingo, writing in her diary or whatever else she's doing, and Rosie, sitting on the other bed, steals glances at her closet. She's seen inside Lena's closet lots of times. There must be a million sequined costumes, but her favorite is the gold lamé head-to-toe body suit with tiger stripes.

What Rosie wouldn't give to be her!

Then, the shoes! On shelves under the costumes, Lena's dance shoes are poised on the boxes they came in. Black patent leather tap shoes, old and new, a white pair with red and blue stars, a glittery silver pair with high heels, and then a basket full of ballet slippers in both black and flesh-tone pink. *What would it hurt if I just tried on a pair of the old tap shoes*? Rosie never asks.

One day, Rosie rides her bike to the church to practice her piano lesson, and on her way home, stops at Lena's house, slips around to the side window of the garage where Lena practices, and spies on her. Rosie studies her steps, her hand movements, even the expression on her face, trying to imagine herself tapping those rhythms. Lena sees her peeking, dances her way to the window, and without even looking at Rosie, pulls the shade all the way down.

Gee whiz!

Since then, Rosie shows up at Lena's house, uninvited, first thing every morning. She sits on the cool concrete stoop next to the lilac bushes, enjoying the sweet scent and listening for voices through the screen door. She doesn't dare knock too early because Lena's dad sleeps late, but when she hears them up and about, she screws up her courage and knocks on the door. When Lena's father comes to the door, he always says Lena is busy, but when Miss Ursula answers, she invites Rosie inside.

Miss Ursula is always doing something, but she stops whatever it is to tell anyone who will listen about Lena's recitals. In the living room, a whole wall is devoted to Lena's pictures in her sequined costumes, a few even in color that show off her lipstick and rouge, and her blue, blue eyes. In some of the pictures, her arms are outstretched and she has a big smile on her face, like a movie star, while in others she assumes acrobatic or dance poses. The most striking is the full-color picture of her in the gold lamé costume, stage bedecked with potted palms, doing the tiger stand pose.

Miss Ursula narrates the wall of photos, pointing out Lena in each of her recitals, in groups or solo, as Rosie stands at attention. She goes on and on about how Mr. Richard loves Lena, saying, "Doesn't he, Lena?" even though Lena isn't in the room. No matter how many times Rosie hears the stories, she gazes at the pictures and obediently nods her head.

It's a Saturday, and Rosie overhears her mother talking on the telephone to Lena's mother, making arrangements for Rosie to spend the day with them. Saturdays are Lena's tap classes at Mr. Richard's! Rosie's never been to a dance class—let alone Mr. Richard's—so she bolts out the door, hollers a goodbye to her mom, and speeds off on her bike.

By the time Rosie knocks on the door, Miss Ursula is already packing Lena's suitcase. Then, she mixes up a jarful of M&M's, raisins, and peanuts for the break, as she says, "So poor Lena doesn't get too hungry."

They walk the three blocks to the bus stop to catch the morning bus to the city, and ride all the way downtown in silence. When they get to the dime store, Lena reaches up and pulls the wire to signal the driver. Miss Ursula gathers up her purse, the suitcase, and the jar of goodies. The three of them file off the bus and make a beeline for a door around the corner. Rosie follows Lena and her mother up the flight of creaky stairs and through the open door at the top.

Inside the room, Rosie stands transfixed.

A mirror covers the front wall, and on the back wall, three gaping windows open to the street below. An old, beat-up upright piano with *Hamilton* written in gold script above the keyboard occupies the far corner, and next to it stands a rickety fan, oscillating noisily and blowing toward no one in particular. The air in the room is heavy with cigarette smoke laced with exhaust fumes wafting in through the open windows. The studio is abuzz with the coming and going of girls and their mothers.

Miss Ursula is yammering at Rosie about the mothers who don't stay for lessons. She says, "I always do, so there won't be any falderal."

Rosie turns toward her, squints and pushes up her glasses to see if she's missed something. *Falderal? What is that?*

Miss Ursula soon joins the others around the table in the adjacent room, and the dancers disappear through a door labeled "Dressing Room." Rosie doesn't know where she should be, so she chooses a place to stand along the back wall in the corner so she can see the dancers' reflections in the mirror.

She watches as the girls reappear, chatting and giggling, wearing colorful shorts over black calf-length tights, clutching their shiny tap shoes and white socks. Within a few minutes, all of the girls are sitting on the floor in their places putting on their taps.

Lena comes out alone, ignoring everyone. She sashays up to the mirror watching herself swing her hips, Marilyn Monroe style. She gets up real close to the mirror, primps, fluffing her blond hair, inspects herself, front and side, looks over her shoulder, and gives her behind the once-over. She watches herself do a tap step several times, then crosses her arms and stands surveying the other dancers through the mirror.

On their feet again, the girls are still animated and engrossed in themselves, oblivious to the clacking and scraping of their shoes punctuating their conversations. Rosie loves the sounds they make, even when they aren't trying.

As if on cue, the dancers begin positioning themselves in two staggered rows, each girl eyeing herself in the mirror. As they find their places, a tall boy in tap shoes and long black pants strides into the studio from the stairway and takes his place on the end of the second row, right behind Lena.

Finally, a woman enters from the stairway. She glides across the room, pointing her toes with each exaggerated step, long black skirt flowing behind her. Her bright red lipstick has bled into the wrinkles around her mouth, and a colorful scarf made into a cloche covers her hair. She settles onto the wooden stool—the kind with a seat that lets you twirl around—in front of the piano, then scoots a little closer to the keyboard.

Rosie can't take her eyes off the woman. She plays some fast finger exercises, and then swivels the stool sideways, crosses her legs, and lights a long brown cigarette. She sits staring out the window, eyes glazed over, puffing on the cigarette and blowing smoke out of her nostrils.

Minutes later, out of nowhere, a man who could only be Mr. Richard himself appears in the studio. Everyone stops talking, and in one move, the woman at the piano uncrosses her legs, puts her burning cigarette into an ashtray that's perched on top of the piano, swivels back to the keyboard, and plays a rising *glissando* followed by a ta-da chord on the piano. The dancers all laugh, and a noise, something between a sigh and a squeak, escapes Rosie's mouth. It is then she realizes she'd been holding her breath.

Other than the piano player, Mr. Richard is the only one not wearing tap shoes—his shoes more like ballet slippers. He stands front and center, also facing the mirror, one eye squinting above a burning cigarette hanging from the corner of his mouth. His nose is nestled between the two deepest crevices of his weathered face, and his bleached-blond hair with dark roots is unkempt, as if he's just gotten out of bed. His black t-shirt is stretched tight over his chest with a cigarette pack rolled up into one sleeve.

In a gravelly voice, Mr. Richard finally speaks. "Warm ups, hoofers! Step to it! Darlin' to the center." He smiles at Lena and his eyes scrunch into two sunbursts of wrinkles. Lena returns a knowing smile to Mr. Richard, and bounces out of line to the center next to him. She faces the dancers.

Rosie is breathless. *He called her Darlin'!*

Mr. Richard gives the orders, "Seven paradiddles—dig, brush, step, heel. Stomp the finish on eight." As he starts the count, everyone stands with their tap shoes quietly poised. Lena stands with her hands on her hips, watching Mr. Richard.

He looks at the piano player who starts playing as he counts, "One and two and red-eye, go!"

The dancers bring their hands to their hips and start tapping. Rosie imitates Lena, with discreet motions, to help herself remember the steps for later.

"Cramp rolls! One and two and red-eye, go!"

Again, they follow Lena's lead—hands at their sides, tapping. Right toe, left toe, left heel, right heel—really fast. Mr. Richard walks around the edges looking at everyone, and sometimes he dances too, his feet silent, calling out different steps to the students.

He barks cues Rosie doesn't understand. "Shuffle-ball-change! Right flap! Spank it!"

She watches in rapt attention, trying to memorize the dance steps. But it all happens so fast, she can't even see what they are doing, much less remember it. Finally, she stops trying, and instead, leans against the wall and feels the old wooden building shaking to the rhythmic pounding of forty feet.

When they finish their warm-ups, Mr. Richard holds out his arms, palm down, motioning the dancers to sit. He nods to the piano player again and says, "Soft-shoe, maestro!" and she plays "Singin' in the Rain."

Rosie is on cloud nine! *He dances like a dream. Is he looking at me? No, maybe not.*

When he finishes, everyone claps, and he stops them, saying, "OK! Everyone up! Back in line. Randy to the front!"

Randy, the tall boy, skips up to Mr. Richard's side. Mr. Richard put his arm around Randy and whispers to him for a few seconds. All the while, Randy is nodding his head and smiling. As Mr. Richard walks away, Randy starts showing everyone the first steps of a new routine. While Randy is teaching the dancers, Mr. Richard walks into the mothers' room right past Rosie without seeming to notice her and pours himself a mug of coffee. He slides back by her, looks at her and nods, "Why aren't you dressed out today, Chickie?"

She is tongue-tied. *He doesn't even know I'm not a dancer.* She shrugs her shoulders. Everything after is a blur. The routine is too complicated for her to follow, so she sits on the floor and watches.

On their way home on the bus, Rosie sits next to Miss Ursula, and Lena sits up front by herself. Miss Ursula talks on and on about Lena and how she always gets to go to the front of the class, how she's the best dancer there. Randy only gets to help because he's Mr. Richard's friend. Then she puts her hand over her mouth and snickers.

Rosie works up the courage to ask Miss Ursula, "Are you going to throw away Lena's old tap shoes? I mean, the ones that don't fit anymore? I get money for helping Mrs. Swank with housework, so I could buy them. I'm only talking about the real old ones?"

She waits what seems like forever for an answer, and finally Miss Ursula sniffs, "Those old things? Who would want someone else's old used-up shoes?"

Rosie's face burns and her ears roar. She spins around to face the front, wishing she could crawl under the seat. They ride the rest of the way home in silence.

That afternoon at home, wearing her black patent leather Sunday School shoes, she tries to do the steps she saw at Mr. Richard's. It just isn't the same. There is no sound at all, so she can't even tell if the steps are right.

On Monday morning, Rosie is back at Lena's doorstep, but this time, Miss Ursula announces through the screen, "Lena is practicing her tap, and later, we are going to Toledo to Lena's cousins' house for the week."

Rosie retreats slowly, drawn to Lena's shaded practice window by the sounds of tapping to the strains of "Glow Little Glow Worm." She pauses to listen, and wonders what she will do all week with Lena gone. As she stands there, Miss Ursula comes out of the house and walks toward her with a deliberate stride, carrying a shoebox. She thrusts the box into Rosie's hands, all the while frowning and shaking her head, as if to say this isn't what she wants to do. "Here," she says, "and don't tell anyone it was me who gave you these old things."

Rosie knows exactly what is in the box. She is so excited, all that comes out of her mouth is, "Huh-uh, no ma'am, huh-uh."

As soon as Miss Ursula turns to go inside, Rosie hops on her bike and pedals like crazy, clutching the shoe box to her chest all the way home. She flings the bike down in the grass by the front door and runs inside, opening the box as the screen door slams behind her. Sure enough, they are Lena's old patent leather tap shoes, a bit worn, but the taps on the bottom are perfect. She runs into her bedroom and grabs a pair of white socks, pulls the socks and shoes on, and ties the frayed ribbons. They're a little big, but that doesn't matter one bit.

She marches around the kitchen floor. The tap sounds are muffled on the linoleum, so she goes out to the sidewalk. *This is more like it!* She counts and taps. She listens with utter joy to the clicking and scraping of her shoes on the concrete, imagining herself on the stage in one of those sequined costumes. With Mr. Richard!

Rosie knows her mom doesn't want her dancing, and Miss Ursula doesn't want her to tell anyone about the shoes, so all week, as soon as Rosie's mom is out the door to go to work, Rosie puts on the shoes and practices tapping. She starts with paradiddles, then tries cramp rolls and shuffle-ball-changes. She practices for hours, then invents her own steps while twirling first one way, then the other. She is in heaven!

One rainy afternoon, Rosie gets her mom's umbrella out of the closet and does her shuffle-ball-change step all the way down the sidewalk while crooning "Singin' in the Rain," just like Gene Kelly does in the movie. Her mom used to have a 78 of "Singin' in the Rain," but Rosie had dropped the record and it had broken into a million pieces.

Her mom was so angry. "Never touch my 78s again! Ever! Money doesn't grow on trees, you know!"

On Saturday mornings, Rosie usually goes to the church with her mom to practice her piano lesson while her mom meets with the Ladies Circle. This particular morning while she is practicing, Mrs. Hoopendorfer (the grown-ups all call her Hoopie) comes into the music room and shuffles through a stack of papers. When Rosie finishes practicing each song, Hoopie claps, then bellows on and on about how nice the song is. Hoopie gets really close in Rosie's face and hollers, "What is the name of that song? Is it from 'Teaching Little Fingers to Play,' Rosie?"

Rosie's mom says Hoopie shouts at everyone when she talks, not because she is mad, but because she's old and hard of hearing. But when Hoopie leans over her close to her face, Rosie has to turn her head because the old woman's breath always smells like the limburger cheese her dad eats.

Rosie stutters and stammers, "No ma'am. Uh, I mean, thank you, Miss Hoopie. It's called 'To a Wild Rose,' though."

"What say?" Hoopie cups her hand to her ear, then before Rosie can repeat her answer, Hoopie continues, "Say, Rosie, we're having a talent show at the Flag Day ice cream social a week from Wednesday. Why don't you play that number in the talent show? Or you could sing. Or both! You have such a gift, Rosie!"

When Rosie hears "talent show", she sees herself on stage, not playing the piano or singing, but tap dancing, just like Lena. She enunciates very slowly, so Hoopie can hear her without getting too close. "Could I do a tap dance instead? For the talent show? I have my own tap shoes now."

Hoopie looks surprised, says, "Oh my! You can tap dance too? Well then, of course, dear."

Rosie walks home with her mom, thinking the whole while about dancing in the talent show. She wishes she could tell her, but her mom doesn't want her dancing, and besides, she works at the market until 6:00 on Wednesday, so she wouldn't even get to see the show. She figures since Miss Hoopie sort of asked her to tap dance, it would be okay with her mom too. All the same, she doesn't mention the talent show or the shoes.

As soon as Rosie's mom leaves for work on Monday morning, Rosie is in her tap shoes, ready to practice. Realizing she needs some music, she looks through a stack of records in the cabinet under the phonograph player. Rosie knows she shouldn't, but she takes Hoagy Carmichael singing "Ole Buttermilk Sky" out of its cardboard sleeve, carefully holds it between her palms without touching the grooves, just like her mom does, and puts it on the spindle of the old RCA Victor in the living room. Then, being very careful not to scratch the record, she places the needle at the beginning of the song, turns it up loud, runs out to the sidewalk, and does some shuffle-ball-changes and paradiddles, the only two steps she can really do.

Each time the song is over, she has to run back into the house and carefully reposition the needle, then run back out to start the dance over. She wonders what a buttermilk sky is, but it doesn't really matter. She likes it—especially the part about, "You can if you try. Don't tell me no lie." And it's just the right speed for the steps she can do.

It isn't long before she knows the song mostly by heart, so she just sings it instead of running back and forth while practicing. She can even hear the violins in her head while she sings the words.

Little by little, she invents her dance. She worries over her hands, holding them out to the side, on her hips, or swinging them back and forth until she finds the motions she likes with each of the steps. Finally, she thinks she'll do a cartwheel or two to end it.

It's Wednesday, and Rosie is ready for the show. Before she leaves the house, she finds her mother's crimson lipstick in the medicine cabinet, carefully applies some to her bottom lip, and rubs her lips together to smear some on the top. Then, remembering how her mother does it, she dabs a small dot on each cheek and smears it around for rouge. Checking herself in the bathroom mirror, she clasps her permed hair to one side with a barrette, puts on her glasses, then gives herself a nod of approval.

She walks the three blocks to the church wearing her costume, a homemade teal taffeta skating skirt with underpants to match, white baby-doll blouse, white nylon socks, and Lena's patent leather tap shoes clicking and clacking with each step.

On the way, she stops several times to try her shuffle step just to hear the taps on the sidewalk but carefully clutches the 78 record of "Ole Buttermilk Sky" in its cardboard sleeve to her chest.

Just as she walks by Phillip's house, he comes out the front door, "Hey Rosie! Where you going, girl? You have on tap shoes?" He is smiling, she thinks because she is dressed up for the show.

"Hi, Phillip. Yeah. See you later!"

Rosie did not want to talk about the shoes, because Miss Ursula asked her not to. Now, she wishes she hadn't worn them and her costume for the walk over to the church. She sure hopes Phillip doesn't talk about it to anyone, especially her mom.

Rosie arrives early at the church, but people are already there setting up tables for the ice cream social after. When Hoopie sees Rosie come in the door, she takes a step back, looks at Rosie's face, and bellows, "Gracious! You're all dolled up!"

She leads her to the room where the young performers eventually gather to wait for their turns on stage. She shows Rosie the record player on the side of the stage, and instructs her to put her record on the spindle when it is her turn. She will be the last act in the show.

The talent show opens with a quartet—four girls Rosie knows from Junior Choir at the church. They pick up their notes from a pitch pipe, then sing "Whispering Hope" in two-part harmony. Rosie sings the low part along with that song at home, so she joins in (discreetly) back stage.

The second act is a boy, David, in a black cape and hat doing a magic act. Most of David's tricks don't work, but no one seems to notice. They still clap when he's done.

Third, an older girl, Addie, comes out in a gold and white satin costume and white boots with gold tassels. She puts her Sousa march record on the phonograph spindle, then struts onto the stage pumping her baton up and down. She twirls it back and forth, throws it up in the air and catches it. On the next throw, she misses, and it bounces off the stage where a little boy is sitting. She just keeps marching in place while he brings it back up to her. She smiles at him, takes the baton and twirls some more.

Next to last is one of the Bell sisters singing "I Believe" a cappella. She didn't intend it to be a cappella, but at the last minute, no one can find her piano player, so she just stands up and sings it anyway. No one gives her a starting pitch, so she pulls a note, one that was much too high, right out of thin air. By the time she gets past the part about hearing a newborn baby cry, it is so unbearably high it's clear she'll never make it to the even-higher "I believe" part that comes next. So, right in mid-phrase, she simply adjusts the pitch downward so she can finish.

Rosie stands in the hallway just outside the stage door listening to the song, and can hear the problem. Holding her fragile 78 record by the edges between her hands so as not to smudge it, she peeks through the crack in the door to see Evelyn Bell on stage. She can't see the audience, but she can see the look on Evelyn's face and knows she is close to tears. When she finishes, the audience claps politely, but Evelyn bolts off the stage, not even taking a bow, and runs straight into Rosie, knocking the fragile record out of her grip. It happens so quickly, there is no time to catch it or break the fall. "Ole Buttermilk Sky" hits the floor and shatters. Rosie doesn't utter a sound. She just looks at the broken record in horror, knowing her tap debut is over and she is in deep trouble with her mom for taking the record to the church in the first place.

Miss Hoopie is tip-toeing to the stage just as "Ole Buttermilk Sky" is tumbling to its demise. She scoops up both girls, one in each arm, and with her limburger breath, whispers that she'll fix it. She lets go of the girls, shuffles to the Sunday School room adjacent to the stage, grabs another record and, breathless, brings it back to Rosie while the audience waits patiently. She slides the record out of its jacket, centers it on the spindle, drops the needle on the spinning record, and pushes Rosie onto the stage, motioning her to begin her dance.

Rosie is now standing in the middle of the stage, hearing the opening strains of Patti Page singing "Tennessee Waltz." It is way too slow. She has no dance for this. She feels the stinging of tears in her eyes as she looks at the floor, blinking hard so no one will see. She walks over to the phonograph player, takes the needle off the record in mid-phrase, lays her glasses on the turn table, and walks back to the middle of the stage with great resolve. She opens her mouth and starts singing, "Ole Buttermilk Sky! I'm keepin' my eye peeled on you..." It doesn't matter that everything is a blur.

She begins to dance. First the shuffle-twirls, then the paradiddles, and so on. She can hear some murmurs from the audience, though she can't see who's out there. It only encourages her to sing louder, "What's the good word tonight?"

The louder she taps, the louder she sings, and pretty soon, she can hear the violins in her head. She does lots of paradiddles and twirls right and left while shuffle-ball-changing, and then starts over. She forgets some of the words, so she skips over those parts and goes right to the verse that says, "You can if you try! Don't tell me no lie. Are you gonna be mellow tonight?"

She sings it twice. When she's ready to end the piece, she does a cartwheel and runs off the stage.

Rosie doesn't notice the applause and the hoots from the audience. All she can think of now is that she'll have to tell her mom everything. About the tap shoes, about the talent show, and about "Ole Buttermilk Sky." And she knows she'll have to do housework all year to pay for the record. She grabs her glasses, then bolts down the stairs past Miss Hoopie, who gives her a thumbs-up, when she runs smack-dab into her mother. Her mother reaches out and grabs Rosie's shoulders, then stoops down and looks right into her eyes. Rosie is paralyzed. She knows she is in deep trouble. She isn't sure what is worse—dancing or breaking the record.

She can only keep repeating, over and over, "I'm sorry for dancing and for dropping the record, Mom. I'll pay for it. I swear!"

When she finally stops for a breath, she is surprised to see that her mom doesn't even look mad. In fact, a hint of a smile is playing on her lips, and she is saying, "What gumption! There's my own daughter, Rosie, on stage, just like a movie star, singing and tap dancing like Gene Kelly! Imagine that!"

She takes Rosie's hand in hers and says, "We'll worry about broken records tomorrow. Right now, I'm thinking about that cherry pie I saw! What do you say we walk on down to the social and have a piece of cherry pie a la mode—that means pie with ice cream on the top!"

"I know."

As they walk away, Rosie wonders again about a buttermilk sky—what that is. Not the song—the sky.

The Vase

As usual, Jon is in the bathroom yelling over the running water, "Why can't she use one of the costumes in her closet? Look at it! It's full of 'em. How much, Ursula? How much more are you going to spend on sequins and tap shoes?"

She knows he can't hear her, so she says it out loud, "Sure Mr. Tough Guy. When she sits in your lap and does her Daddy-this-and-Daddy-that thing, you never say no."

Ursula continues silently—*You didn't have a problem spending two thousand seven hundred and sixty-four dollars on a brand-new Buick. And you bought that before the ink was dry on the check from the Navy. Besides, Norman loved his baby sister. He would have wanted her to have whatever she desires.*

Now Jon is yelling because he doesn't have a fresh razor blade. He storms into the kitchen, naked, chin covered with lather, holding his open razor, no blade, up in the air, and spouting, "Can I get some attention around here? Who the hell brings home the paycheck?"

He retreats, slams the bathroom door.

Ursula, mildly amused by the sight of him, unwraps the soup bone and drops it into the pot of boiling water on the stove. She scrubs some potatoes, more vigorously than necessary, then chops them, relishing the whacking noise as the knife hits the Formica.

In the beginning, she and Jon wanted lots of kids, but after Donald and Norman were born, she lost a baby girl, four-and-a-half months into her pregnancy. Heartbreaking. They didn't think she could have any more kids. But then Lena surprised them some five years later. Being the only girl in the family as well as the baby, Lena has been pampered by everyone, especially her big brothers. In fact, Ursula worries she will be so spoiled she will never find a man who will put up with her. *I guess we've all spoiled her.*

Ursula dumps the chopped spuds into the broth, sets the pot to simmering, then picks up her garden scissors and steps out back into her early summer garden. Norman's old Cocker Spaniel, Happy, strains on his tether and barks wildly at the sight of her. *Salt in the wound.* Seeing him every day reminds her of when Norman was a boy, how Happy would wait with him for the school bus in the morning and then be at the stop in the afternoon to walk him home—every single day, rain or shine, sleet or snow. He grieved when Norman left. Now, she wishes someone would just take the old dog away.

On her way to the dill patch, she cuts a bunch of zinnias for the small vase on the table. Norm always helped her plant the variegated zinnias. Then, he would turn on the sprinkler, purposely getting himself soaked, to give them a drink, as he liked to say. Weeks later, as he watched them push their heads up through the garden earth, he'd guess the color of each bud. Zinnias were always his favorite.

She takes her time in the garden, stopping to check the tomatoes and okra on her way to the dill patch. Some will be ready for picking and canning in a week or so, but today they just need watering. She snips the dill for the soup and is comforted to hear Lena's rhythmic tapping in the garage. *Life goes on.*

Before returning to the kitchen, Ursula reaches down and turns on the spigot to the sprinkler hose. It begins pulsing in its meter, spraying the tomatoes and the zinnias alike. Happy settles back into the doorway of his dog house, out of the water spray, keeping his vigil. *He's not coming back, Happy… Happy?* She wishes his name was anything but Happy.

In the kitchen, Ursula arranges the multi-hued dwarf zinnias so they stand tall in the celadon vase, providing a colorful canopy for its carved dragon. The vase was a souvenir Norm sent from Korea. It had arrived after they got the news. Jon told her she shouldn't use it because it might get broken, but she brings it out anyway when the mood strikes her.

She jabs a potato with her cooking fork and nods her head in approval. The soup is close to ready, so she scrapes the beefy scum off the top and adds a handful of dill sprigs, releasing the gentle fragrance into the kitchen and the distinct flavor into the soup. *How Norman loved my dill soup.* She would always poach two eggs in the dilly broth for him—he liked his yolks runny—and he'd slurp it up while Happy waited for him just outside the screen door.

She pulls the kitchen towel from her apron pocket and dries her eyes.

"What are you up to this afternoon?" she would ask Norm. He would just shrug his shoulders and when he finished eating his soup, he'd yell, "Thanks, Mom! You're the best!" on his way out the door. He was such a good kid. His older brother Donald was a good kid too, but Norm was his mother's boy.

In the days after the news came, she blamed Jon, though she didn't tell him then. Not until the first anniversary of Norm's death, in May, just a month ago. She was inconsolable that day.

Through her tears, she had blurted it out, "If you hadn't signed for Norm to go into the Navy when he was 17 years old, I'd still have my boy."

Jon's face had gone red with anger. He stood up, edged around the table until he was standing over her. He yelled, "Don't you ever say that again, woman!"

Shaking his fist at her, he raged, "There was no god-damned Korea when I signed. But he died defending freedom and his country. He died fighting the damn Commies! And he wasn't just your son, Ursula. He was my son, too."

He broke down into sobs like he hadn't before. She could not console him.

They had never had words like those before. Never.

Now, for the most part, she and Jon go about their business in silence. She puts his supper on the table every day at one o'clock sharp. She mindlessly performs her housewifely chores while he eats to the sounds of Lena tapping on the cement floor, or when she's at school, to the sound of silence. Always the same routine, Ursula sends him off with his lunch bucket and thermos to his second shift job on the assembly line. On his way out, if Lena's there, he opens the kitchen door to the garage and she gives him a good-bye hug. It's the only time Ursula sees him smile anymore.

Ursula relishes having the afternoon to herself. She sits down at the table and strokes the vase that holds the zinnias, closes her eyes as her fingers trace the carved dragon. Its surface feels crackled, splintered under her touch.

She wonders if her boy had cried out for her.

A knock at the door distracts her just before the tears flow. *It must be Rosie. Rosweeta! What a pretty name*! Ursula can see Rosie worships Lena. All the kids do. She comes by almost every day, sometimes sitting on the front stoop, waiting for Jon to leave before she knocks.

Ursula stands up, calls toward the door, "Jiminy Crickets, Rosie! Have you been here all this time? Well, come on in. Have some dill soup and keep this old Bohunk company."

Jon used to call her his little Bohunk, then he'd give her a slap on her rear and wink at her. They don't touch anymore.

Ursula pulls out a chair and motions for Rosie to sit, and she quietly obeys. Ursula picks up the vase of zinnias with both hands, carries it into the living room, and sets it down on the end table next to the picture of Norman, the one where he's in his sailor's uniform looking like a grown man and not the boy he had still been when the picture was taken.

Back in the kitchen, Ursula re-lights the stove under the soup pot, then takes an egg from the Frigidaire and cracks it into a bowl. She stands, arms crossed, waiting for the soup to boil.

"Do you like your yolk runny, Miss Rosie?"

"I don't know, Miss Ursula. Whatever you do is okay with me."

When the soup is steaming hot, Ursula turns off the burner and lets the raw egg slide from the bowl into the soup. After a few minutes, she ladles some soup into a large bowl, then scoops up the poached egg and gently floats it on the broth.

"Norman likes…liked…his runny," she says in a whisper.

Rosie nods, but says nothing.

"Soup's hot. Careful, girl."

Rosie smiles and nods again and says, "Thanks ma'am."

They sit together at the table, Rosie slurping the dill soup to the sounds of "Glow Little Glow Worm" and Lena's tapping coming from the garage. Rosie's fingers are keeping the beat, and Ursula is gazing out at the back yard, watching the spray from the hose twirl round and round.

Ursula breaks the silence. "Did you know your mother well, Rosie? I mean your real mother? Before....?"

"I know what you mean. No. Not really. I mean, not much."

Ursula has never pried or asked questions about Rosie's background, though she has always been curious. She continues, "But you didn't live with her—your real mother—did you?"

"Well, yes. I mean, no. I lived with her sometimes, but not..."

"Why didn't she keep you, then?"

Rosie stirs her soup, creates a whirlpool with the poached egg twirling in the center. Her eyebrows drawn into a deep wrinkle, she answers, "I don't know."

Ursula can't imagine how a mother could give away her daughter, or son. *Rosie is such a sweet girl. How could a mother do that?* She wonders if Rosie ever cries for her mother the way she does for her son.

Rosie slurps the poached egg from her soup spoon and nods, approvingly. The music in the garage stops and Lena bursts into the kitchen from the garage. She doesn't acknowledge Rosie—just looks past her, asks her mother if she can quit now. She says Phillip is coming over to practice for cheerleading tryouts, and dashes off to her bedroom.

Rosie watches Lena disappear into her room. "I'd better go now," she says, as she scoots her chair away from the table. "And thanks for the soup, Miss Ursula." She slips out the back door, and Happy barks expectantly again.

Ursula leans against the door jamb, watching as Happy knocks Rosie over with his exuberant jumps, then licks her face clean while she laughs and tries to fend him off. *It doesn't seem right that the zinnias come up again, the sprinkler continues to turn, and Happy still is.*

Why me, Lord?

Harold dreads going home. Not so much the going as the being there. He loves his wife, or whatever is left of her, so he hopes against hope that his taking the twins to her brother's house for an extended stay will make a difference for her. Still, he wonders if it will. And then, what? *I'll still have a job to do to support my family, and I still won't know what to do with a wife who won't even take care of her own babies.*

"Why me, Lord? Why me?"

It's still quite early in the day, a beautiful early summer's day, when he pulls into his driveway. He steels himself to face Doris—takes a deep breath, opens the front door. He is overwhelmed by the darkness, the stale cigarette air, the utter mess. He opens the shades in the living room, and sees Doris lying, back to him, on the sofa. She doesn't acknowledge him, but his last hope vanishes only when he walks into the kitchen and flips on the light. He can only describe it as filthy.

He stands at arm's length from the sink. It is still overflowing with dirty plates, coffee cups, bowls of half-eaten cereal. Dirty pots are stacked precariously on the stove, one with the residue of pork 'n beans, and an iron skillet with an unrecognizable crust burned onto the bottom. Several empty soup cans and a half-used pack of hot dog buns in an open wrapper rest where they had landed days before he left. Harold, reaching over the dirty dishes, opens a cupboard door, looks into the empty shelves, then slams it shut.

"Criminy sakes, Doris! I can't even find a clean cup for my Nescafé. I told you before I left to call someone in to help you clean this place." He turns toward her, arms held out in a questioning gesture. "Have you even moved from the couch since I left?" He turns back toward the kitchen. "It's even worse than before I took the twins to your brother's, and that was three days ago! Nothing in three days? I thought they were the problem and that if they weren't here, you could take care of the house?"

He walks into the living room where she still lies slumped on the couch, looking at the floor. He watches as her fingers pick fuzz from the blanket, roll it into a tight ball, then drop it onto the floor.

He begins to fume. "I know you're not right Doris, but gee whiz! Can't you get your behind off the couch long enough to wash a dang cup? Can't you even say hello to your husband?" He starts to walk away, then he turns back. "I guess not. If you can't even take care of your own babies, why would you say hello to me or get up to wash a cup?"

She sniffles.

Harold, confused and near tears himself, paces back and forth from the kitchen to her. She's lying on the sofa, whimpering.

"I'm sorry, Doris. I shouldn't have said that. It's just… I don't know what on earth to do. Tell me what to do!" He kneels down and grips her shoulders, pulls her up so he can look into her eyes. "Those two sweet boys stood at the door, crying for Mommy, watching me leave."

"I know…" she looks down and cries, "I'm terrible…I'm not…"

"Stop it!" His finger under her chin, he pulls her head up so she is looking directly at him. "I'm pleading, Doris! This is not about you. It's about our twins, those two darlings who don't have a mother right now." He releases her, letting her crumble onto the sofa.

"I know you think I'm awful because I can't …" She sobs, repeating over and over, "I'm sorry. I'm sorry, Harold."

"You've got to snap out of this Doris. It's like you don't even love those boys! What happened?" He doesn't move—still looking into her eyes, hoping for her denial.

"Everything is about the twins…they always need something, or want something. No one…no one…cares about me! I can't do this, Harold!"

He withdraws from her, staring at the floor.

Doris continues her desperate plea, "Maybe I'm not meant to be a mother."

"What? It's a little late for that, don't you think? You wanted those babies. You *are* a mother and those babies *need* you. You don't have a choice!"

Now standing, Harold unleashes his frustration. "Look at me, Doris. Look at me! We talked about this. I know you don't want to go, but I'm taking you to see Dr. Edelman. He's a shrink, a head doctor. Doc Smith tells me your problem is mental, and I should take you to see Edelman. Otherwise, he says he'd just put you into the mental hospital. The looney-bin, Doris. So maybe Dr. Edelman will have some other trick up his sleeve."

Doris nods. She takes Harold's outstretched hand, and he pulls her up off the sofa. "This just isn't right, Dorie.

And it *is* all in your mind, you know. With some help, we should be able to get it out of your mind. Right?"

She looks at the floor and nods. Harold puts his arms around Doris and holds on for a long minute. She begins to cry, and Harold struggles to hold his own tears.

"You need to get cleaned up and I'll call Dr. Edelman's office." He moves her toward the bathroom. "How many days without a bath? And your hair— golly sakes!—it's all tangled. You get your bath, Dorie, and wash your hair. Then put on something decent. And clean."

He steps into the bathroom to get the water started for her bath, but stops and turns to her. "Good God, Doris! This place smells like a sewer! Look at that pale of diapers— they stink to high heaven! When were you planning to do laundry?"

She opens her mouth to answer him, but says nothing. He stomps out of the bathroom, slams the door.

Harold waits, sits across the living room staring at the withered rose petals that have fallen to the floor, the remnants of a bouquet that he had brought home for their anniversary—when was it?— weeks and weeks ago.

Her voice floats past him. *Everyone would be better off without me.*

He isn't sure she actually said it or if he just imagines it, but it frightens him. He rests his head in his hands, covers his eyes, thinks about Doris—who she was before this evil thing gripped her mind. *Will it ever be the same with us?*

Dr. Edelman's nurse opens the door and peeks her head out. "Mr. Swank, can you come back for a moment? We'll be right with you, Mrs. Swank."

Harold looks at Doris who nods, and he follows the nurse's directions. "The doctor would like to talk with you for a minute before he sees Mrs. Swank. Just go on into his office."

Dr. Edelman wastes no time. "So, Mr. Swank. Before I talk with your wife, please sit down and tell me what's been going on, why you're here today."

"Thanks, Dr. Edelman. First of all, let me say, my work requires me to be out of town several days most weeks, sometimes more, so I'm not always home to see what's going on. But here goes." Harold makes eye contact with the doctor, who nods for him to go on.

"Our twins (they're two and a half)—they're the only reason she gets out of bed in the morning, but they're also the problem for her, I think. But anyway, now they are gone. I mean, not gone-gone—but they're with her brother's family. Temporarily. And the house? She's done nothing at all in the house—you wouldn't believe it. It's a gol-dern mess."

"Most of all, I'm worried about the kids, when they get back. Sometimes when I come home they're dirty, diapers need changing, and I can't even tell you how disgusting the kitchen is. Who even knows what they've had to eat."

"So I took the twins, day before yesterday, to spend the summer with her brother's family in Mayfield, to give her a break. She didn't even want to go with us."

"A break from what? Sounds like she's taken a break from the children already?"

"Yes. You're right. She's not taking care of herself either. I thought by taking the twins to her brother's house—her sister-in-law and ten-year-old niece are willing to help—she'd get herself together. But when I came home this morning, the house looked worse than when I left with the twins. She was on the sofa, crying and saying she's no good and maybe she shouldn't be a mother. Oh, and she said everyone would be better off without her."

"Is she taking any medications?"

"Yes, I think so. She takes some pills to sleep. She says she can't sleep, but when she takes her pills, she sleeps all the time."

"Anything else I should know before she comes in?"

"Just that everyone knows that she's not been herself…"

"Let me interrupt a minute. Who is the everyone you refer to? Her parents? Are they close by?"

"No, sir. They are not. Her dad isn't around and her mom doesn't visit. She and her mom have had some kind of tiff. I was thinking of her friends, but she doesn't have many here. She's a loner, pretty much. We haven't lived in Springdale that long."

"Okay. Go ahead with what you were saying."

"Everyone knows that she's not been herself since the twins were born. Even Doc Smith knows. She's been up and down, taking sleeping pills to help her, as he says, 'to cope with life as a mother.' He calls it post-partum depression, whatever that is. A new thing they're talking about now, I guess."

"One last question—Has she ever tried to hurt herself or the children?

"You mean….? No, not that I know of. Huh-uh. No."

"Alright, Mr. Swank, I'd like to talk with your wife alone, then the three of us will sit together to decide where we go from here."

"Yes, I'll wait out there. One last thing—this is the worst it's been. Right now. And it's more than two years since they were born."

Dr. Edelman stands and he nods.

Harold sits in the waiting room for what seems like forever before the nurse calls him back in. He can tell that Doris has been crying. He pats her shoulder and bends over her, whispers, "It's okay. I'm here."

He moves toward the doctor, who speaks to him in a low tone, "It seems that your wife has a nervous condition, and it could be because of the children, but post-partum problems usually start earlier. Depression is its own thing. Lots of ways it plays out."

Looking at Doris, he brightens up. "In any case, I think a prescription for Miltown, we call it 'mother's little helper'..." he smiles at Doris, "...that should do the trick. It's effective and should help very quickly. Take them as directed." He adds, "We'll keep you on the sleeping pills for now, strictly for nighttime, but eventually we'll wean you from those. And I would like to see you regularly to monitor your mood and continue our therapy sessions." Doris is frowning, but nodding her head.

He speaks confidentially to Harold, "If these don't work, we do have electric shock therapy that we can try. Sometimes it's the only thing that works for them."

Harold glances at Doris and notes the pain that flashes across her face.

Edelman continues, looking at Harold, "People don't like the sound of that, and I don't blame them, but it isn't as bad as it seems. And if that doesn't work or we decide against it, we may choose to institutionalize. To protect her from herself. But let's just cross those bridges when we get to them. That alright, Mr. Swank?"

"Yes, sir. Thank you."

"Do you have any questions, Mrs. Swank?

Doris shakes her head and mouths her answer, "Not right now."

Harold and Doris drive home in silence. Once in the house, Doris lights a cigarette and retreats to their bedroom. Harold fumbles around in the kitchen looking for a glass, then abandons his search and says to the open bedroom door, "I'm bringing your pills that the doctor gave you. Don't take any sleeping pills until tonight, though. Okay?" He takes the few steps to the bedroom door. "Where is your glass? Oh, there it is. Here, take one," and tosses her the bottle of mother's helpers.

"It's getting on, Doris—I need to go to Goodman's to get some things for dinner and breakfast. I also need to stop by the office and get my schedule for next week. But first, I think I'll go ask Rosie, across the way, to come in and help you get the house in order, okay?" He raises his hands to the door as if to ask for some kind of response. Then, hearing none, he heads out, letting the door slam behind him.

He remembers the last time Rosie came over to clean up. He was home and watched her in action. *Heck, she did the dishes, scoured the pots and pans, and put them all away—all while keeping the toddlers busy. Then she tackled the living room—toys littering the floor, overflowing ashtrays, kids' clothes draped over the furniture.* Rosie made picking up their toys a game for them, which he had never seen anyone do. By the time Rosie left, everything was in order and the twins were laughing.

It sure feels good—finally tackling Doris's problems head on. I know Rosie will be darn happy to come over and help, and make a little money to boot. She's such a nice kid and so mature for her age.

Harold returns to the house with Rosie and announces them. "Hey, Dorie! Rosie is here to help. She'll be in to see you in a minute, but I'll get her started out here."

He starts giving Rosie instructions but can see right away she knows what she's doing, so he sets her loose in the kitchen. It's music to his ears to hear dishes and pots being stacked and scraped, water running, Rosie humming.

He checks on Doris and sees that she's either asleep or resting with eyes closed, so he opens her window for fresh air and leaves, pulling the door to.

"That's great, Rosie. You go ahead and deal with the kitchen, and I'll get some fresh air in here."

He opens a window, and then another as he chats. "Doris will sit all day in this closed up house, smoking and staring at the wall."

"And where's everyone?" asks Rosie over the sound of silverware rattling.

"Oh, the boys are in Mayfield, Rosie—just for a while."

"Is it okay then if I turn on the radio?"

"Sure thing, Rosie. I'm going to town in a minute. I'll be back in an hour or so. Need anything from Goodman's?"

"No. Nothing I can think of. You could call my mom and she'll bring it home for you, so you don't have to go, that's if you want."

"That's okay, Rosie. I need a break and I have to go by my office. I'll be back in an hour or two. If you finish, just let Doris know…oh, never mind. Here, let me just give you your money now so you can leave whenever you finish. Is two hours good—a dollar, right?"

"Sure, but…" she pauses, "is Mrs. Swank sick?"

"No. Well, yes, sort of. But she'll be better soon, I think."

The radio comes to life and Rosie giggles at the jokes and sings along with the songs.

Harold realizes now how terribly unhappy his home is, and has been for so long—especially with the twins gone. No laughter—just emptiness.

He heads out to run his errands, hopes that Doris will be more normal by the time he returns, but he knows it may take longer. He stops by Goodman's, and Rosie's mother is behind the butcher counter. She smiles and nods. *She's always so pleasant!*

He responds with a smile and tells her, "Your daughter is at my house helping Doris. She sure is a great helper!"

"Oh, is Mrs. Swank under the weather?"

"A bit, yes… a bit. But the twins are visiting Doris's brother, so Doris can rest."

"Um hmm. That's good. What can I get for you today?"

Harold feels awkward. He doesn't really know Rosie's mom that well. And people don't talk much about family that goes mental.

He stops at his office for a while before heading home. His work schedule has him traveling next week—he had hoped he'd be able to stay home, but this is such an important client.

When he gets home, everything is quiet. And clean. *Thank heavens for Rosie.*

He goes into the bedroom, looks at Doris—she's still out. His jaw tightens. "Doris? You awake?"

She responds, slowly opening her eyes.

"When's the last time you took a nice walk, Doris?" He is exasperated. "Did you take your new pill?"

She nods, pulls herself half-way up.

"Can you tell anything? How do you feel?"

"Same."

He sits on the edge of the bed. "Come 'ere, Dorie." He puts his arm around her, pulls her close and rocks her, gently. Tells her again that he loves her and he just wants to help her. "I just don't know what else I can do." He pauses, rocks her again. His voice takes on a desperate edge, "You know the Doc says the only thing left to do is to shock you with electricity. You want that? They damn near electrocute your brain! If that doesn't go well, they put you in the looney-bin. Then what about the twins? What am I supposed to do, Doris?" His voice cracks. They hold each other and sob.

She tries to answer, "Please don't... don't..." but the tears start to flow again. "I miss my babies. I do. I'm so sorry, Harold. I can't...I'll try..."

He doesn't blame her. He knows she really wishes she could just snap out of it, as he says.

But he doesn't understand—he has to ask... "Why haven't you even called them? At least do that, Doris. Call the twins, or call your sister-in-law, for God's sake!" He rests his head in his hands. "I told them we'd be down to see them soon. As soon as I can get a break, the end of next week, we'll go. Okay?"

She nods, flops back down in the bed and still the tears flow.

"Honey, you remember the doctor said you won't feel better right away, right? C'mon. Let's give the pills time. I have a good feeling about his pills. For now, I think we should take a nice walk and get some fresh air."

They walk, hand in hand, to the park. She sits on a swing and Harold smiles, pushes her ever so gently. "Little by little, Dorie. We'll get there."

"I love you, Harold."

Cheers!

Phillip Lee Fever picks up on the second ring and, certain it's Lena, announces, "Philippe le Fièvre at your service, Madame!" He affects a French accent, as he often does when she calls, and ends his greeting with a newly acquired lisp.

But it isn't Lena on the other end. It's Lacey Boyles, that girl with the mean, vulgar mouth. She always says something ugly to him, starting their usual exchange of insults and name-calling. "Why if it isn't Phil-eeep," she sneers, emphasizing the eeep, "our very own commie-fairy majorette!"

Phillip grimaces at the receiver, then barks back, "Jealous? I heard when you tried out for majorette, the judges all laughed!"

Phillip shoots off more insults in rapid fire, then ends with, "Lice-y? Why don't you just get lost?"

"My brother says you're a fairy. A queer." Lacey continues, waiting for a response. Hearing none, she goes on, "Oh, and by the way, Lena wants you to prance on over here to her house and practice some queer cheers."

He raises his voice, "I don't speak with one-celled organisms. Put the Princess on the line."

The telephone goes dead—he gets a dial tone, "Damn Lacey! Did you hang up on me?" He hates it that she gets to him.

He dials Lena's number which, of course, he knows by heart. Someone picks up. He hears muffled voices, then Lena speaks, "Give me the phone. Go outside, Lacey. Go on. Get out of my bedroom. Wait outside. I'll get in trouble if Mom sees you in here."

Lena speaks into the receiver, affecting her best Scarlett O'Hara accent, "Phillip, dahling! Ah'm just going to scuh-ream if you don't come over raht now!"

Phillip worships Lena. Everyone does. But he is not in the mood for Scarlett. "What's she doing there? I said I'd try out with you, Lena—not her!"

"Come on Phil, you know I didn't invite her. She just shows up. Please! Tryouts are in two weeks!"

"Okay, Lena, but get rid of her." He drops the receiver into its cradle.

Both Phillip and Lena take advanced acrobatics from Mr. Richard, so they easily perform the cartwheels, jumps, and splits required for leading cheers on the basketball court. Lena, going into her junior year, is cute and a natural for the squad. She made varsity for the past two years, so no one doubts she'll be picked again. She was the youngest varsity cheerleader they've ever had on the squad.

Phillip, on the other hand, tried out last year, and though everyone said that he was just as good as Lena, he didn't make the squad. The sponsors were surprised that he even tried out, as he was the first boy ever to compete, and they couldn't imagine why a boy would want to be a cheerleader. They recommended that he try out for drum major to lead the marching band instead, which he did, and he was chosen. He'd still rather be a cheerleader, and as this is his senior year, he won't get another chance.

Phillip turns the corner onto Lena's street and sees them in the yard. Lena executes a perfect cartwheel. Lacey tries, but her body looks awkward, legs going every which way. As he approaches them, Phillip turns his face away from her, pinches his nose between his thumb and forefinger, and mouths, "P.U."

Lacey scowls at him.

Lena, saying nothing of their silent exchange, says to him, "Good! You're here. Let's do some cheers!"

"Okay, Lena. Let's warm up."

He deliberately keeps Lacey behind him, and then looks over his shoulder at her and, under his breath, says, "Hussy."

She hisses, "Queer."

Phillip, his back still to Lacey, says to Lena, "Straddle split stretches."

He steps back while Lena slides effortlessly into a half, then a full straddle split, arms extended, palms facing up. Lacey tries the split, too. Sliding halfway down, bouncing a few times, trying to go further but cannot get all the way down. She doesn't make a sound, but Phillip delights in seeing her face contort as her lips form an "ow!"

While he rolls his shirt sleeves up to mid-arm and re-tucks the red and white striped shirt—school colors—into his freshly ironed white pants, Lena does three perfect back walkovers in a row while Lacey gawks at her, hands on her hips, looking like she's going to cry.

"You still here?" he says to Lacey. No answer. She stares him down.

Phillip looks down at Lacey's bare feet. "Where are your shoes?" He doesn't expect an answer and he doesn't get one. Just a look.

"OK paper shakers, then let's do some jumps."

He crouches slightly to prepare the jump, then, up he goes, arms and legs fully extended, his meticulously polished saddle oxfords just grazing his palms. Of course, for Lena it's easy too—she's already an accomplished cheerleader. But when Phillip sees Lacey's attempts, he doubles over laughing.

Lena is in her own world doing other moves, but when she hears him laughing at Lacey, she turns toward him to see what's so funny. "Phillip!" she scolds.

Phillip asks, "What?" Then to Lacey, he says, "Show us your herkie."

Lacey frowns and cocks her head to one side.

He erupts in a loud, overblown laugh. "If you don't know the moves, why are you even here? Nobody, but nobody, is going to vote for you. And you're not trying out with us. Period."

Just as Lena is in mid-jump, her mom steps out on the porch and calls her in for lunch. Lena motions to Phillip to follow and the two of them walk toward the front door. Phillip feels Lacey's eyes piercing his back, but he does not look back.

Lena's mother, holding the door open for them, welcomes Phillip. "Come on in. Want a sloppy Joe?"

"Sure, thanks, Miss Ursula."

When the door closes, she asks about Lacey. "Who is that girl out there, Phillip? Is she the one who lives in that junky place on the Hills Road, right behind you? Because I don't want Lena running around with her. Those people are filthy and they steal your things if you let them inside your house. Look at those tight shorts and that skimpy halter. And no shoes! Doesn't she even have respectable clothes?"

Phillip leans toward Lena and silently mouths, "See?"

Lena shrugs her shoulders and sits at her place at the table. Her dad is already eating, and her mom sets another place for Phillip. She gives them each a sloppy joe on a big hamburger bun, fried potatoes piled on top.

Lena's dad mumbles, "Where's the ketchup?" Her mom gets the bottle of ketchup from the Frigidaire and sets it in the middle of the table, then continues to fuss around the kitchen while the three of them eat. Her dad unscrews the lid and pours an ample puddle of ketchup on his plate, then screws the lid back on and sets the bottle on the table. Phillip, who can think of nothing to say, reads and re-reads the ketchup label while he eats. He's happy to have lunch, but honestly, he can't get away fast enough.

Back at home, Phillip is all set to spend the afternoon, as he often does, listening to records and practicing his dance routines. He likes being home alone—no one to please but himself. And sometimes, he pretends that Randy, Mr. Richard's assistant, is there dancing with him. He is so in love with Randy. He thinks about him absolutely every minute of every day.

For now, he doesn't feel like dancing, so he lies on the couch and entertains random thoughts about his feelings, his life, his future. Randy is all he can think about. *Randy is so... so gorgeous. His body. His mind. He dances like a dream!* Then, his mood shifts. *There's nothing to do in this stupid town. Randy doesn't even know I exist.*

Phillip goes into his bedroom to retrieve one of his magazines from under his mattress. He takes it into the living room and flops back down on the couch, fingers the magazine and thumbs through the pictures in the book. He thinks about his plans to go to Los Angeles when he graduates high school. He's read that they started a new thing called the Mattachine Society to give guys like him a place to go.

After a time, he decides to do one of his favorite things—polish his shoes—his saddle oxfords and his white bucks. And ironing. He loves to iron his clothes.

After tending to both pairs of his shoes, he drags the ironing board out of the closet and into the kitchen, sets up the iron, and retrieves his dampened clothes from the refrigerator. He turns on the radio to the music station and picks his blue pin stripe shirt to iron from the clothes bag. He has a method for ironing shirts that his sister taught him which he uses without fail—first the collar, then the yoke, the two fronts, the back, then the sleeves. "Perfect!" He hangs it up on a hook in his bedroom.

Slim Whitman is in the middle of singing *Indian Love Call* when he hears a commotion in the back yard. He looks out his back door and is about to open it when he hears a shriek and sees, over the fence, Lacey running toward his house, her mouth open in a scream and her face distorted. Her top is torn and she's barefoot, running through the clods of dirt and overgrown weeds. Giving chase right behind her is the meanest and biggest of her brothers—the one who had called him queer and threatened to run him over with his truck. "If I ever see you on a lonesome road," he had said, "you'll be roadkill."

Phillip opens the screen door to step out toward her, but stops, still holding the door open.

Lacey scrambles toward the fence and tries to vault it, but her brother snatches her up, hits her across her face, and yells, "Shut the hell up!" his oversized hand now covering her mouth. Silenced, the desperate plea in her eyes meets Phillip's. The brute turns toward Phillip. "What are you lookin' at, you fancy-ass queer? I'm after you next!"

Phillip steps back and lets the screen door slam shut. For a moment, he stops breathing, then gulps for air. All he can do is look on in horror while Lacey is carried back through the field. He hears her scream for help, and they disappear into the trailer.

Phillip latches his screen door, then quickly closes and locks the inside door. His heart is racing and his mouth dry. He is no match for any of them. He stands at the kitchen window, scouring the back yard for any of the brothers, having no idea what he would do if they came after him.

Standing by the open window, Phillip hears a long low wail coming from the trailer. Then, nothing. He feels his throat tighten and his eyes blur with tears.

Creeps! Half yelling, half-sobbing, he hastens to the living room, checks the locks on the front door, closes the Venetian blinds, then paces from the living room to the kitchen and back again. He stops and stands at the kitchen window, paralyzed, watching the trailer for any movement. He tries not to think about Lacey. Anyway, he has no idea what to do about her. She's not the same as the other girls, like Lena and even Rosie. Plus, he doesn't even know which brother it is. Their names all start with O—Owen, Otto, and Olin, which everyone thinks is weird. And they are all horrible. He wonders what she did to make her brother so mad.

The phone rings, startling him out of his paralysis. He raises the receiver to his ear but says nothing, afraid that it might be the brother.

"You there, Phillip?" It's Rosie's voice.

"Rosie?"

"Yeah. Can I come over? Can you show me some acrobat stuff?"

"Oh my God. Something horrible just happened. Come right away to the front door and be sure to yell your name. I'm not coming outside."

"Why? What happened?"

"It's about Lacey. Just hurry. I'll watch for you."

In no time at all she is at the front door, knocking and yelling her name at the same time. Phillip opens the door a crack just to verify that it is Rosie, and she quickly pushes her way in, shutting the door behind her. Phillip locks the door, then ushers her to the back, relieved that someone is there with him, even if it is just Rosie. Still unable to explain why, he keeps repeating in a crescendo, "Oh my God, oh my God, oh my God! Rosie!"

Phillip twirls around, then holds his head between his hands. His face is twisted into a grimace.

Now Rosie is shouting, "What? Phillip? What happened?"

"Okay, okay."

He swallows hard, starts pacing back and forth in the living room.

"Here goes, Rosie. You're not going to believe this. I shouldn't even tell you because you're so young. But you seem older than you really are. So here goes. Lacey's brother chases her out the back door, across the field, and then grabs her, hits her, and carries her back to the trailer."

Phillip is gesturing wildly, pointing to the back door.

Rosie is frozen in place, sees the fear in his eyes. She holds her hand over her mouth. Only her eyes follow Phillip as he continues to pace back and forth. "Then what?"

"They both see me looking, Rosie. Her shirt is ripped almost off her and there is someone else there holding the door open to the trailer. And this is the worst part. Her brother tells me—Oh my God—he tells me he's coming after me next."

Phillip stops pacing, looks down. He doesn't say anything to Rosie about the desperate, silent look in Lacey's eyes as her brother carried her back to the trailer. And he doesn't mention the scream he heard coming from the trailer.

"Geez, Phillip. Weren't you scared?"

"Are you kidding, girl? I was terrified!"

He grabs her by the shoulders and gets in her face. "I'm scared to death!"

Now Phillip paces back and forth from the kitchen to the living room, while Rosie stands guard at the kitchen window, eyes fixed on the trailer door.

"What should we do, Phil? I mean, what if he comes over here?"

"I don't know! I'll get in trouble if I call my mom at work. Anyway, what can she do?"

"Maybe we could go down to Goodman's and talk to my mom. I mean, if she doesn't have customers. Anyway, he can't get you if we're in the store. Right?"

"My dad will be home at supper time. I could just wait here if you stay with me and tell him what happened. He doesn't like those people at all. But my mom is always saying I shouldn't bother him, so maybe we should go down to Goodman's. Or we could go to Lena's house and see what she thinks."

"Well, I don't know, but I think we oughta go talk to my mom. What if he comes over here? Come on."

The two of them leave through the front door, and they run the whole first block toward the downtown, not even stopping to look back. And then Phillip says, "Oh my God, Rosie. I forgot to lock the door!"

With that, Rosie starts laughing and soon is bent over, laughing hysterically. Phillip grabs her arm and yanks her close to his face and tells her to shut up. She stops the hysterics and Phillip tries to look nonchalant as they walk into the store.

Rosie's mom is behind the butcher counter and greets them. "Well, look what the cat drug in! I'm surprised to see you here. What's up?"

"Hi, Mom. We're just taking a walk."

Phillip is looking at the candy rack, fingering a bag of M&M's.

Rosie continues, "Actually, we thought maybe if you're not too busy we could get a malted or something at the diner?"

Dottie looks from one to the other, and Phillip can tell she knows something's up. "You want me to go, too? Right?"

Rosie nods.

"Okay. Hold on a minute, kids." She opens the door to the back room and hollers, "Mr. Goodman? Can you watch the front while I take a break with these two youngsters?"

Goodman, always soft-spoken, nods and smiles at Rosie. "Sure thing, Dottie."

Her mom takes off her apron and hangs it by the meat case.

"Come on. Let's go."

The diner is two doors down from Goodman's, and it isn't usually busy at this time of day. They find a booth and promptly order two malted milks—Rosie likes chocolate, Phillip orders vanilla. Rosie's mom has a mug of coffee.

Dottie watches them across the table. Phillip fidgets with the salt shaker, and Rosie drums her fingers on the table.

"So, what's going on, kids?"

Phillip puts down the salt shaker, starts to open his mouth, then stares straight ahead.

Rosie looks at him, then at her mom. "It's about Lacey, Mom."

"You mean that awful girl over in that rundown trailer? You two aren't running around with her, are you?"

"No, Mom, no. Listen! One of her brothers hit her in the face and forced her to go back to their trailer. Carried her back! Phillip said her blouse was ripped, too. She was trying to get away and she was screaming for help. I wasn't there, but Phillip told me all about it."

Rosie's mom looks at Phillip for confirmation. At first, he shrugs his shoulders, then he nods his head. "That's right. And he said he's coming after me next. Because I saw the whole thing!"

"Good heavens, Phillip! Where were you?"

"In my house. At my back door. Because she was screaming. I went out to see what about."

Rosie chimes in, "She was screaming and trying to get over the fence when he hit her. Her halter was ripped almost off, right Phillip?"

The girl behind the counter turns on the malted machine which makes so much noise they can hardly hear each other, so Rosie's mom is yelling over the noise.

"Phillip, I'm sure your mom has already told you a thing or two about those people. They're filthy. Mind you, you don't know what she did to provoke him, to make him hit her and carry her back inside. I know what you're thinking, Phillip, but girls often lie about those things. You don't really know what she did to make him so mad!"

Rosie looks at Phillip, then at her mom. "Lie about what things? What about Phillip? He didn't do anything to her brother."

Her mother avoids the questions.

Still yelling over the din of the malted machine, she warns them, "Don't get involved, neither one of you, with that..."

Just as she is finishing, still yelling, the malted machine shuts off, spewing her last two words of advice all over the diner. "WORTHLESS TRASH!"

The waitress spins around to look at Rosie's mother, obviously thinking she is calling her a name. Rosie's mom just shakes her head no and puts her hand over her mouth.

The waitress delivers the malted milks to Phillip and Rosie, with only a sideways glance at Rosie's mother. Phillip can't look at Rosie's mom now without wanting to laugh. He just glances at Rosie, and he sure isn't going to tell her mother what Lacey's brother said to him. He and Rosie give each other a knowing look, then sip vigorously on their straws. The only thing anyone hears after the outburst is that grating, bubbly noise made when they suck up the last drops of their malted milks.

Phillip thanks Rosie's mom and he and Rosie walk in silence the few blocks back to his street.

"What are you going to do, Phillip?"

"I don't know."

As they approach his house, Phillip digs deep in his pocket for his key, then remembers, "I didn't lock the house! Merde! What if he's in there?"

"He won't be in your house. What's merde?"

"It's cussing in French. You can say it because no one knows what it means."

"Huh?"

"Oh, nothing."

"You want me to wait out here until you go in?"

"And then what'll you do, Rosie? If I run back out, he'll be chasing me."

"Okay then. Do you want to come to my house?"

"I can't go and leave my house unlocked, Rosie. My dad will put me on restriction. He already hates me."

"Oh Phil, he doesn't hate you. So, okay. When does he get home? We could just sit out here like we are just talking and stuff, so you won't get in trouble. And if Lacey's horrible brother is in there, and he comes out, we can run."

They sit in the lawn chairs positioned to watch both the door, in case he comes out, and also anyone coming or going on the sidewalk. Only there aren't many people coming and going this time of day, so after a few minutes, Phillip decides to circle the house, looking in all the windows. Before he rounds the corner of the back of the house, he stops to look at the trailer to see if anyone is outside. No one. Then he slips around to the kitchen door to peek into his house. No one's in the kitchen or living room that he can see. He doubles back to the front and signals an all clear to Rosie.

"I'm going in. If I scream, run home and call the police, okay?"

Rosie grimaces, and puts her hand to her mouth. He tells her to move to the edge of the yard to have a better vantage point for running, if she has to.

Phillip opens the screen door, trying to be very quiet, then opens the front door a crack, peering in. When he sees nothing unusual, he opens it further, and further still until it is wide open and he's standing in the doorway. He turns to Rosie, now emboldened, and says, "Nothing so far. Stay there and listen for me. I'll go inside."

After a minute, he comes back to the front door and motions her inside. They both go to the kitchen to look at the back yard and the field, wondering aloud what happened in the trailer. There is no sign of anyone now.

Phillip thinks about what Rosie's mother said about not getting involved and that you don't know what Lacey did to make him do whatever he did to her. Maybe he shouldn't even tell his father. He'd have to say that the brother called him a queer. He didn't even want to say that word, queer, to his father because he hates those kinds of men.

Anyway, he doesn't like Lacey, not one little bit. In fact, he thinks she's totally disgusting. And he thinks she probably did do something to aggravate her brother.

He looks at Rosie, "Let's just put on a record. I have a Nat King Cole album. That okay?"

"Sure. But Phillip. Shouldn't we tell someone? What if they really did something to her?"

"You heard your mother, Rosie. Who can we tell and what would we say?" He looks through the record jackets, pulls out "Unforgettable" and puts it on the spindle.

"What if they had come over here? To beat you up?"

"That's different."

"I don't know, Phillip. If they hit her in the face…she might need help."

"And if we say anything, they will come over here. And then I'm dead!"

They sit on the sofa, neither of them speaking, listening to Nat sing…

Nobody's Child

Lacey stands barefoot in her shorts and halter on the back step of the trailer, taking in the stillness of the morning and relishing each small bite of her Twinkie. It's a bright summer day, and outside it smells all innocent, fresh. No one around to spoil it.

Her attention is drawn to two raucous blue jays flitting back and forth from a low-hanging oak branch in her yard to the clothesline in Phillip's yard where freshly laundered sheets hang as a backdrop to the pink peony bush now in full flower. She tip-toes to the edge of the field, then through the clumps of clay and broken corn stalks, trying not to call attention to herself, to get a closer look at the birds, so beautiful in their bright blue plumage. They sit on their newly claimed perch and call and preen and call some more, then fly away. She gets a whiff of peony perfume mixed with a slight scent of bleach, and wishes she lived in a house that smelled of clean sheets and flowers.

Back in the trailer, she goes into the kitchen to make a baloney sandwich. She opens the fridge, fishes for the baloney and sees the crumpled bread wrapper next to it. No bread. Again. Shit. She'll have to go to the laundry to get money from her mom for bread. What she does not want is to be here when the creep wakes up.

Owen's her half-brother. Half the time he doesn't even get dressed. Half-wit. He just sits around in the recliner with his fat hairy belly spilling over his BVD's, a Schlitz in one hand, snorting and reaching for her with the other. He likes to snap her bra and bellow, "Show me your boobies!" then laugh like a hyena. She manages to avoid him, mostly.

Outside the front door, she circumnavigates the old rusted out 1939 Pontiac Chief that has rested there on blocks since before she can remember. Her bike, a boy's model with a broken kick-stand and no fenders, sits propped against the Chief's back door, between a pile of rusted appliances, random furniture parts, and other yard junk. Still barefoot, she grabs the handle bars and gets a running start, mounting from the left and slinging her right leg over the seat. The bike has no brakes either, so stopping really hurts if she's not careful.

She stops first at the school playground where she squeezes onto a swing, idly watching some little kids on the merry-go-round. She remembers second grade, her favorite teacher, Mrs. Becker. *When she talked to me, she would always put her arm around my shoulder and pull me toward her. I loved how she made me feel back then.*

It's a long ride, at least ten minutes, to go to Sunshine Laundry and Dry Cleaning just for bread money, but Lacey doesn't want to ask the lady at Goodman's to let her mom come in later to pay. She'd probably say, "Again?" Plus, she didn't have anywhere else to go, so she might as well ride uptown to the laundry. Riding her bike, she could just dream about Roy. She purrs softly, "Roy loves Lacey." *I wish.*

Lacey does wish she had the kind of mom she could tell about Roy, but, of course, her mom wouldn't like it at all if she knew she'd been going with him in his truck. Especially not what they did there. She'd probably get a good beating.

She first met Roy that time when her tire went flat. She had walked her bike to the filling station with the front tire as flat as a pancake. He was washing some guy's windshield. When he finished, he came right over to her with the air pump and pumped up her tire. He was real nice to her that day.

"Not sure if it will hold," he had said, so he didn't charge her anything. And he called her "young lady!"

A few days later, she was riding to the station and saw his truck coming down the road toward her. He stopped and hollered, "Get in." She dropped her bike right where it was and slid into the front seat. Once they turned off of Main, he pulled her over close to him. He took her hand and she was on cloud nine, but then he mashed it down hard on his zipper and told her, "Go ahead. Unzip it." So she did.

He turned the truck into the cemetery and stopped, then pulled her close. As she lifted her face, making her mouth ready for his kiss, he pushed her head down into his lap and turned off the ignition.

Now, she stops by to see him most days, and sometimes, after he gets off work, he takes her for a ride. She loves the smell of his truck. He's a real mechanic, all right. She wonders what it will be like to marry Roy and have babies. Whenever they ride in the truck, since that first time, they always end up at the cemetery. He tells her he likes her, but he never does kiss her.

Like yesterday.

When they were coming back from the cemetery, she asked, "Do you think we could go steady, Roy? I mean, I don't need a ring or nothing. If you just say…"

He interrupted, "I like you better when you don't talk, kid."

Her face flushed, and she brought her hand to her mouth as if to muffle the sound. Even thinking about that now makes her face feel red hot again.

When her mom's boss at the laundry sees Lacey riding up to the door, he leans out of the service window and barks, "Whad'ya want, kid? What's with the red face? You need some water?"

She tells him she needs a quarter for bread money from her mom, please. He slides a quarter out of the cash drawer and flips it up in the air for her to catch. He says he'll get it from her later. She thanks him, doesn't ask to see her mom.

Riding back, it's earlier than usual, but she thinks she'll go by the filling station anyway. As she turns the corner, she sees Roy outside laughing and talking to a woman with blond hair and high heels. He walks right past Lacey without saying anything. He acts like he doesn't even know her. When she follows him to the office, he tells her, "Don't be hangin' around here," and slams the door in her face.

Her throat seizes up as she chokes back tears. *Don't I do it right?*

She rides on down to Goodman's Market for a loaf of Sunbeam for sandwiches, and buys the bread and a Hershey bar with a penny to spare. Even though she needs to take the bread home, she sits on the curb and takes her time eating the Hershey bar. Still sucking on the last square of chocolate, she decides to ride down Lena's street to see if anyone is outside. As she turns the corner from Phillip's street, she sees Lena in the side yard doing acrobatics, so she rides up, props her bike against a tree and drops the bread next to it. When Phillip comes over, they practice their cheerleader routines for the tryouts while Lacey watches. She wishes she could learn cheerleading, but no one will ever show her how to do it, and Phillip tells her to "get lost!"

When Lena and Phillip go inside for lunch, Lacey has nowhere to go but home. She rides past the schoolyard to her dirt road, balancing the loaf of bread on her handle bars, hoping the creep won't still be there. Sometimes his friends come to get him and he'll be gone for a couple of days or even a couple of weeks.

She swings her right leg back over the tire, grabs the boy bar while holding the bread wrapper in her teeth, and coasts on one pedal up to the Pontiac, stopping herself by getting hold of the car's aerial—a move she's proud of. With bread now in hand, she threads her way through the junk piled up by the car, then pushes open the door.

There he sits in the recliner, staring at her. *At least he's got his overalls on.*

"Well, well. Come in, little sister, and make us something to eat." He lets out a loud, deliberate fart while sneering at her.

"Make it yourself." She throws the loaf of bread at him, and, careful to stay out of arm's reach, sidesteps across to the kitchen. She can handle him.

Just then, Smitty appears in the bedroom doorway. *Two of them?* She freezes.

Smitty is her mother's boyfriend. He hasn't been here since school was out. He hauls freight in his eighteen-wheeler whenever he can get a load, and when he's here, his truck is always parked just outside.

"Where's your truck? Does Mom know you're here?" She edges toward the back door.

Smitty's eyes narrow. "Your mom doesn't need to know everything. I got somethin' here just for you." He starts undoing his pants.

Owen gets up and now they both move toward her.

Owen chimes in. "Yeah, let's give her a twofer. Something she can brag about." Leering at her, he makes slurping noises.

As he fumbles with the buttons on his coveralls, he moves between her and the front door. She eyes her path to the back door, past Smitty, who's moving toward her. When Smitty is almost close enough to reach her, her adrenaline kicks in and she bolts for the back door. He misses her, but catches her halter and she hears it rip just as she flings herself through the open door. She sprints for the cornfield, screaming and trying to hold her torn halter on. *Faster!* She hears Owen close behind.

He yells, "I'll get you, you little whore!"

When she reaches the fence, she sees Phillip standing in his kitchen doorway, watching her. *Help me!* Her eyes meet Phillip's, pleading. He opens his screen door like he's going to come out and help her, but he stops. Stands there motionless. Just as she gets one foot in the fence to hurdle it, Owen reaches her. He rips her from the fence, and hits her face, hard, then claps his oversized hand over her mouth.

Owen turns to Phillip, "What're you lookin' at, you fancy-assed queer? I'm coming after you next!"

Phillip takes a step back and allows the screen door to slam shut.

She bites Owen's hand, and when he yelps and lets go, she screams toward Phillip again, "Help me!"

Owen grabs her hair and yanks her head back. "Shut up, slut!" Then carries her, arms and legs flailing and kicking all the way to the trailer.

Smitty holds the door open, watches the spectacle, a menacing smile on his face. "We got a fighter on our hands, eh?"

Inside again, Owen hefts her into the bedroom and throws her on her mother's bed. She curls to a fetal position. Now, there is no one to stop them. Owen says, "You know you want it. You look like a slut, prancing around here in these." He grabs her feet, pulls her legs straight ,then yanks off her shorts. He starts undoing his overalls.

Smitty, behind him, cuffs him on the back of his head and pushes him out of the way. "Me first, punk."

She covers her face with her hands so she can't see or smell Smitty's putrid mouthful of rotten teeth. *He's a maggot.* She won't look at his thing either. He descends on her, pushes her legs apart, fumbles around, but has trouble, so he helps himself with his own hand. All she can hear are his guttural noises—but at least he isn't doing it to her.

Then the movement stops and he rolls off. She pulls her knees together and tries to get up, but Owen grabs her legs, pulls them apart like a wishbone. "Now for a real man!"

He piles on, clutches her wrists with one hand and pulls her arms over her head, putting his weight on her wrists so she cannot move. With the other hand, he yanks her torn halter and bra up so he can molest her breasts. She squeezes her eyes shut, turns her head away from his nasty beer breath. *Somebody help me!* She knows there's no help for her. He is too heavy and he is savage. Thrusting, plunging, repeatedly until she begs, "No! No! Please!" He laughs and pushes faster, stabbing pain. *He can kill me and no one would care.* At some point, she hears a long, loud wail—*hers?* There are no tears.

He finally finishes.

Smitty, still looking on, says, "You like that, don't ya'? I waited a long time for this! You'd better not be talkin'. You tell your Mom and she won't believe you. She'll run you off. Or you might just disappear, huh?"

She doesn't doubt it. There's nobody for her. She pulls on her shorts and covers her breasts with her hands long enough to get to the bathroom.

Owen follows her to the door and says, like a kid tattling, "So I hear you been goin' to the cemetery with Roy down to the station. Him and the other guys at the station were laughin' 'bout you the other night. He says you're easy. Says you'd do all the guys at the station. Says he can get a gang bang goin' anytime they want. What about it, slut?"

Her face is burning. She can't see anything but red, hear anything but the high-pitched screaming in her ears. She leans over the stinking toilet and pukes, violently. Then she wretches again and again with the dry heaves. He disappears.

She says nothing. Pulls on a t-shirt from the laundry pile. Smitty warns her, again, "Remember Little Girl, if you tell her, she'll kick you out."

She leaves through the front door, straddles her bike, the seat pressing against the stinging, burning between her legs. She rides faster than she has ever ridden, directly to the filling station. She sees Roy, laughing and chatting with a customer, and when he turns to look at her, she throws her bike to the side and makes for him, cursing under her breath. He detours swiftly to the store, but Lacey catches the door before it closes and chases him inside.

Before he can escape, her fists are flying, her fingernails gouging his face, and she is screaming at the top of her lungs, "You lyin' pig, slime-ball, you whore-dog son-of-a-bitch!"

Fighting back, he grabs at her hands, but her fists are flying so wild all he can do is hold his arms in front of his face. Still pounding in the direction of his face, she jerks her knee up, connecting with his crotch. He howls and doubles over, and before he can straighten up, she lands a punch squarely on his left eye. He cries out again, and holding his hands over his face, he twists away from her.

Finally, two of Roy's cronies grab her from behind and pull her off. She's still screaming, "Don't you ever talk about me again, you bastard!" She screams all the way out the door. They shove her outside and she falls to the pavement. She struggles to her feet and staggers to her bike. She's vaguely aware of a small crowd gathering, jeering.

Roy, already exhibiting a bruised eye, sticks his head out the door and yells, "Get outta' here, you crazy bitch! And don't ever come back!"

She mounts her bike, but not before turning to face him with her middle finger extended, and another swear word on her lips. Smarting from the scrapes on her legs, she rides straight to Phillips house, steps off her bike in his front yard, letting it fall in the grass. He had been there in the doorway, behind his screen, watching as Owen carried her back into the house. *He never even tried to help.*

She pounds on his door with her fist. When no one answers, she knocks again, and again. Rings the doorbell. She tries to peek around the edges of the closed Venetian blinds, but can't see in at all. She's so hungry she's shaking and her mouth feels like cotton. She yells in the direction of the door. "Phillip! It's Lacey! Are you in there? Please! Please let me in!"

No answer. She collapses on the steps of his front stoop, head in hands. Still barefoot, she examines the scuffs on her legs and notices blood on the end of her big toe that she doesn't even remember stubbing. She replays the events of this day, over and over, feeling the bile back up in her throat. *I hate them!* She clasps her arms around her legs and rocks back and forth. Finally, angry tears flow, and she sobs uncontrollably. *I hate them!*

After a time, she hears the door latch open, and looks up. As she stands up, she attempts to wipe the tears from her face and smooth her hair. It's Rosie. *What's she doing here?*

She asks, "Where is Phillip?" Rosie looks back into the house, says nothing.

"Bye, Rosie! See you tomo…" Phillip sees Lacey, stops mid-sentence and puts his hand over his mouth.

"Why didn't you help me? I was trying to get away and they…"

He interrupts. "Lacey, I can't let you come in now. Look at your feet, legs. Filthy! Oh my God! My parents would kill me. Or actually, your brother will come here and kill me. Did you hear what he said? You have to go somewhere else. He said he'd run over me with his truck!"

"But I'm starving, Phillip. Can you give me something to eat?"

"Lacey, I can't… okay. Never mind. Wait here." He looks at Rosie, "Will you stay with her? And let me know if anyone shows up?" Phillip disappears inside, closes and latches the door.

Lacey looks at Rosie, but Rosie averts her eyes. After a moment, she says to Lacey, "You can't stay at my house either. I'm sorry, Lacey. My mom doesn't like…" Rosie doesn't need to finish the sentence.

Lacey looks at her feet and wipes away tears with the backs of her hands.

"What happened, Lacey? Phillip says your brother hit you—why'd he do that?"

Phillip reappears with a peanut butter and jelly sandwich and hands it out the door to Lacey. Ignoring Rosie's question, Lacey takes it and stuffs half of it in her mouth, chewing and swallowing eagerly before turning back to Rosie.

She gulps the rest of the sandwich like she'd never see food again. "Can I get a drink of water? Please? I can't go home."

"OK, Lacey, you can come home with me for a little bit. I'll get you some water and you can clean up. But you have to leave before my mom comes home. Okay?"

"I'll do whatever you say, Rosie."

"I'll take her to my house, Phillip. Be sure to let me know if anyone is looking for her though."

Phillip nodded, then closed and locked his door.

"C'mon then. Let's go, Lacey."

They walk past Lena's house. Nobody's outside now. When they get to Rosie's house, she takes Lacey inside to the bathroom, hands her a towel, and runs the water into the tub. "You should take a bath Lacey, but you gotta' hurry."

Lacey nods her head. "OK, thanks Rosie."

When the bathroom door shuts, Lacey sees herself in a full-length mirror on the back of the door. She sheds her clothes and examines her body. Her face a mix of tears and dirt, a hand print across her cheek, soot and bloody scrapes on her legs and feet, bruises on her wrists. A roadmap of her day.

She slides into the tub, warm water stinging all the torn, scraped places, inside and out, and then, soothing. She lies all the way back to get her hair wet, and lets her tears slide into the warm water.

A gentle knock-knock on the bathroom door. "Lacey? It's me. I have some clothes that a lady gave my mom for me. They're still too big for me, but I think they'll fit you, so you pick out whatever you want to wear, okay? I'm going to put them on my bed for you. Only, don't tell my mom, okay? I'll be on the porch. But you gotta hurry, okay?"

In the pile of clothes, Lacey sees a yellow sun-dress with tiny lady bugs on it. She holds it up to her body to see if it's the right size. It's so pretty. She wants to wear it, but she puts it back and takes some pedal pushers and a blouse instead. More practical for riding her bike. And that reminds her of her bike that she left lying in Phillip's front yard. She doesn't want to go get it now, because Rosie might not let her come back. She steps out onto the porch wearing the new pedal pushers and the blouse. She says nothing about the bike.

"Thanks, Rosie. Thanks a lot. For the clothes, I mean. And the bath, thanks for that too. Your bedroom is really pretty, Rosie."

"It's OK, Lacey. And you don't have to thank me for everything."

"OK. Thanks. You're so nice to me, Rosie. Nobody ever…" She doesn't finish.

Rosie turns her face away and almost whispers, "My mom will kill me if she ever finds out you were here."

After a moment, she asks, "What happened, Lacey? Phillip said after your brother hit you, he made you go back inside. Why did he hit you?"

"I can't tell. You don't know them, Rosie. And it wasn't just him. It's Smitty too. My mom's boyfriend. I can't go back there. And if I say what they did, they'll disappear me."

"Disappear you?"

She pauses, looks at her feet. She feels the hot tears again. "Promise you won't tell? Because I'm not going back there. Never going back. Never!"

Rosie nods. "I'll never tell, Lacey. Promise." She holds up the three-finger Brownie promise, then quickly changes it to the two-finger Girl Scout salute.

Lacey erupts into tears, alternately sobbing and recounting the horror. "Smitty and Owen tore my clothes off…" She sobbed uncontrollably.

"Oh no, Lacey!"

"Yes. And then they held me down and forced me. Smitty says…" continuing to cry… "if I ever tell my mom, she will run me off."

"Oh no, Lacey! She wouldn't, would she? Your own mom?"

Lacey nods her head and can't stop bawling. "There's more, and this is the worst part, Rosie. Owen forced me really bad. He hurt my arms, and, you know, he did it inside me."

"Oh Lacey! He did? He made you do it? Oh how awful!"

"Yes. He said it was my own fault, because I was prancing around in shorts. He said I wanted it."

"Did you? I mean, you didn't, did you?"

"No!" Suddenly Lacey is embarrassed and ashamed, regrets telling Rosie. She clasps her hand over her mouth, muffling her sobs.

"I'm sorry, Lacey. I didn't mean to say…"

Lacey and Rosie both turn their attention to an approaching car, and without looking at Lacey, Rosie starts chattering, "Look, Lacey! Here comes Mr. Swank. He lives across the street. Sometimes I babysit and clean up their house. They give me thirty-five cents an hour. He's real nice, but his wife, Mrs. Swank—her real name is Doris—she's sick or something."

Lacey, watching Mr. Swank park and go inside, asks, "What's wrong with her?"

"I don't know. My mom says it's in her head."

Harold is no sooner in his house than he comes back out and hollers over, asking Rosie if she can come over and help Doris out, as he has to drive to Cincinnati tonight.

"Sure, Mr. Swank. Can my friend come over, too? She's real good at cleaning up. I'll show her how to do everything."

"Sure, Rosie. The more, the merrier, I always say."

He turns back and yells through the open door. "Doris? Rosie is here and has a friend with her to help you get things straightened up. Go ahead in, girls. I'm gone for the best part of the week, so you can help Doris whenever she needs you. I'm leaving the front door key under the mat. Be sure to lock it when you finish, and check in on her every day or so, okay? Make her get up out of that bed!"

Rosie takes Lacey by the hand and knocks on the bedroom door. There is no answer, so Rosie pushes the door open a crack until they can see Mrs. Swank, who is propped up on a pillow, smoking a cigarette and looking at them through the crack in the door.

"Can we come in, Mrs. Swank?"

She nods, then, in her usual quiet voice, "Who do you have there?"

"This is Lacey. She's going to help clean today." Lacey pokes her head in the door and gives a tentative wave to Mrs. Swank.

"Bring her in, Rose. You have a very fancy name, Lacey. Where're you from, honey?"

"Hills Road, ma'am."

Mrs. Swank pauses, making eye contact with Lacey. "OK, you two. The kitchen first, then… maybe… supper? We're on our own here, you know. Harold and the twins have all flown the coop." She breaks an almost imperceptible smile then stubs her cigarette in the ash tray. She mouths the word *shoo*, at the same time makes the gesture with her hand.

When Lacey sees the messy kitchen, she makes a face at Rosie. Rosie whispers that it's always like this. "Probably worse because the twins are in Mayfield," she says.

They busy themselves cleaning up and putting away. Nearly finished in the kitchen, Lacey asks about supper. "What do you make her for supper?"

"I have to go home for supper. My mom will be home and she doesn't want me over here at night, plus, I don't want Mom to see you here. Go ask Mrs. Swank what she'd like."

Lacey raps on Mrs. Swank's open bedroom door.

Mrs. Swank looks startled, but turns toward Lacey. "Yes, Lacey. What is it?"

"What do you want for supper, Mrs. Swank? I mean, Rosie has to go home to have supper with her mom, but I don't have to go anywhere. I can cook supper if you want. You don't have to pay me."

Rosie interrupts. "I better hightail it for home now, but Mr. Swank said to check with you tomorrow. Is that okay?"

"Do you want some money, Rose? Who's getting the money?" She looks past Lacey at Rosie.

"It's okay, Mrs. Swank. We can divide it up tomorrow, if that's okay with you?"

"You keep track, Rose."

Mrs. Swank looks off in the distance, and Lacey stands at attention for what seems like a very long time. She hears the front door close, then hears the lock engage. Finally, Mrs. Swank answers. "Whatever's in the Frigidaire or the pantry. Do you know how to cook, Lacey?"

"Yes, ma'am. I cook at home. I make macaroni and cheese, hot dogs, pork and beans, baloney sandwiches, whatever they want. I'll go see what there is for supper."

She almost runs to the pantry, which is just a couple of shelves on the landing between the back door and the basement stairs. On those shelves are cans of home-canned peach halves, store-bought pineapple rings, string beans and Spam, and some macaroni. There are also home-canned tomatoes and saltines, but no bread. She goes back into the kitchen and opens the Frigidaire, looking for something else. There is a smallish mound of hamburger in a carton in the bottom, and three hamburger buns in a package. She picks up the hamburger and smells it—smells okay—and decides to make sloppy joes, her mom's favorite. And maybe some peaches to go with it.

Lacey feels safe now. No one will look for her here. They probably won't even look at all. But she's getting worried about her bike being at Phillip's, plus he knows she went home with Rosie.

She takes her time finding the salt and pepper to add to the hamburger and tomatoes in the skillet, then stands stirring, wishing it was just her mom and her at home. But then every time the memories of the day intrude, she tears up again. She heard Johnny Ray and the Four Lads on the radio the other day. They were singing "Cry" and now the song just keeps playing in her head. She sings softly, "It's no secret, you'll feel better—if you just cry." And she does, again, standing there stirring the sloppy Joes.

"Now young lady, what are you so sad about?"

Lacey is startled to see Mrs. Swank standing in the door of the kitchen. Her hair is disheveled and her dressing gown wrinkled and spotted, but she has the hint of a smile.

Lacey answers timidly, "Nothing, ma'am."

"Now honey, you can't fool an old fool like me. I've been watching you and I can see into your sad heart. I know how a sad heart looks. And I know where bruises come from. Come, sit down with me. Turn off that silly stove. We'll cook later. Come."

They sit down at the kitchen table across from one another and Mrs. Swank takes Lacey's hands in hers and holds them tight. Lacey is anxious. No one in her family ever holds hands. She tries to pull away, but Mrs. Swank holds firmly while smiling at her. She can't figure out what Mrs. Swank means by this, so she looks hard at her, right in the eye.

"Good. You keep looking at me."

With a firm grasp, she turns Lacey's hands over, back and over again, studying the bruises on her wrists and arms.

"Now, first, tell me who did this to you. Who made these bruises?"

Then she lets go, and Lacey pulls back, tucking her hands under her armpits.

"And those on your cheek? Who did that?"

Lacey touches her cheek, almost reflexively, and can no longer hold back. "It was Owen. He's my half-brother. And Smitty, my mother's boyfriend. I'm never going back there, Mrs. Swank! I tried…"

Mrs. Swank interrupts, "Oh my God. Of course not!"

Lacey continues, "But that's not all! I tried to run away, but they caught me and dragged me to my mother's bedroom, then they forced me. Both of them. I tried to get away!" She is crying and sobbing, her voice frantic with fear, "I can't go back there."

"Oh my God! No, no, no. You *cannot* go back there. Where is your mother, for God's sake? Who's child are you?"

Lacey thinks of her mother, but knows she has no one. "Nobody's child."

Mrs. Swank gasps, her mouth tightening into a thin line. She reaches for a cigarette and Lacey watches as she lights it and takes several long draws. She continues, "Are you telling me your mother doesn't live there?"

"No, ma'am. She lives there with her boyfriend and sometimes Owen."

"Call me Doris, okay?"

"Okay, Miss…Doris. My mom works. She's always at work. And Smitty says even if I tell her, she won't believe me. That she'll run me off if I…" Her voice breaks.

"Oh, you poor dear soul. This isn't your fault, Lacey. It is not."

She continues, her voice cracking, "It is not your fault! Even if they get away with it, and they usually do, you do not deserve this. How old are you, honey?"

"I'll be seventeen in August—I'm a senior next year, ma'am."

"Look, you're staying right here. For now. You're going nowhere until we figure this thing out. Does Rosie know that this happened?"

"Yes, ma'am. And Phillip too. He lives in the house across the field from ours. He saw Owen hit me and drag me back to the trailer. He didn't help, but Rosie let me take a bath and gave me these pants and shirt. Mine were dirty and ripped."

"That's nice of her. Rose is a very nice girl."

"Rosie told me that you are sick, and that someone said it's your head?"

There is another long silence. Mrs. Swank snubs out her cigarette and brings her hands together, fingers outstretched in front of her, as in prayer. She seems to contemplate her hands for a time, then looks up.

"Lacey, I'm going to tell you a story that no one else in this town knows. Not even Harold. Especially not Harold. I need you to promise that you'll keep it between us. That you'll tell no one. Ever. Will you do that?"

"Yes, ma'am."

"Call me Doris. Okay?"

"Yes, ma'am. Doris."

"God help me. Here goes." Doris stands up and walks into the kitchen. Pacing back and forth, she continues. "When I was eleven, my mother and brother and I lived with my grandfather. He took care of us while my mother was at work on the second shift. My dad was long gone, so he was like a dad. But he was a monster, Lacey. He molested me. My own grandfather. Not once, Lacey, not twice, but over and over again. He was my mother's father, Lacey. When I told her (I was sixteen then), she called me a liar."

Doris walks back to the table and looks into Lacey's eyes and continues, "The very next day, I left home and came to Springdale with my boyfriend, Billy."

Lacey keeps her eyes fixed on Doris.

"One day, Billy hit me because he didn't like his hamburger the way I cooked it. He almost knocked me down. I promised myself—and told him so—I'd leave him if he ever hit me again. Then, one night, not long after that, he beat me within an inch of my life. My girlfriend Sarah (we worked together) knew what was going on—she saw my swollen face and black eye—and she begged me to come stay with her. Well, I finally did. I left him. And, to make a long story short—after some time, I moved into my own place. Then—well, not right then, but soon after—I met Harold. He's been very good to me, Lacey. He knows about Billy, but I have never told him about my grandfather. Never."

"Now I have twin boys, Lacey, little ones, and I can't even be a mother to them. And I don't deserve Harold. He's so good to me, and I'm useless. I have to get better soon or I won't get my babies back home."

Lacey is overcome with sorrow for them both. She tries to say something, but she just doesn't know what to say.

Doris pulls herself together—looks straight into Lacey's eyes without blinking. "I'm telling you this story, because I know it's lonely as hell being nobody's child—I know what that's like. And I'm here to tell you, those bastards aren't going to win this one, too. We're going to tackle this one together. You and me! You are not alone, Lacey! Never again."

Lacey wants to reach across the table, wants to touch Doris, but isn't sure she should. She wants to tell her that she knows how she feels about what happened to her, but can't find the words. Crying ever so softly, she returns Doris's pledge, "You are not alone either, Miss Doris. I'm here for you."

She sees that Doris, tears streaking her face, is wiping her eyes, and then starts laughing. Now Lacey can't decide what to do, whether to laugh or cry. Doris reaches for

Lacey's hand and says, "Just look at us. Both blubbering like babies! We are quite a sight, you and me, honey."

She takes Lacey's hands, and says, "We're going to be okay. And we don't need to talk about these things any more. Only if you want to. We're family now."

Doris and Lacey stand up together and Mrs. Swank pulls her toward the kitchen, saying, "Let's get those sloppy joes cooked. I'm starving!"

Lacey nods her head, then glances out of the kitchen window just in time to see that Rosie has retrieved her bike and is wheeling it into Doris's shed, out of sight.

"Yes, ma'am...Doris. I'm hungry, too."

Jailbait

Lolling around his house on the sofa on a typical summer afternoon, Phillip retrieves his beefcake magazines from under his mattress and pages through his favorite pictures. He was fourteen when he first spotted *Your Physique* in a corner newsstand in downtown Detroit. It took him three visits, sneaking glimpses of some pages inside, before he had the nerve to buy it. When he took the magazine to the seller, the man asked Phillip if he was old enough. Phillip's first reaction was to giggle, so he put his hand in his pocket and pinched his thigh until it hurt, a trick he had learned from his dad. Then, he cleared his throat and in his deepest voice said, "Yes, sir, I am."

Once empowered, he rolled up the magazine so no one could see the cover, and walked back to his cousin's house where the family was visiting. His first real look at the magazine was in his aunt's bathroom. He hadn't known what "physique" meant until he saw the muscular, nearly naked bodies—pages of them! He still can't describe the surge of emotions that overcame him when he turned that first page. He had never felt so mixed up before. It was desire, pure joy, taking him to a fevered pitch. Then, guilt and shame. He knew what he was doing was wrong—evil, the minister at their church had said. Still, he could not help repeating this act several times that afternoon.

The next day, now braver, he went back to the news stand and bought two more magazines: *Tomorrow's Man* and his favorite to this day, *Physique Pictorial*. When he first opened its cover, he thought he had died and gone to heaven. It was not just a magazine. It was a catalog of pictures of beautiful men caressing other beautiful men! Yes, he knows they are models posing. *But maybe they really are men who love other men?*

Now, his magazines are worn, the torn pages being his favorites that have kept him company over several years. He dreams of what his life will be like when he's old enough to get a real job and move away from this horrible place. *With Randy... I wish!*

This summer, since he met Randy, his life has changed. Randy's a dancer, older than Phillip—twenty or older, he thinks. He's Mr. Richard's assistant. Phillip thinks about him while he's browsing his magazines, when he practices his dance routines, when he listens to his records. In other words, all the time. He finds excuses to go to the studio or stay late after a class. He carries on a dialogue with Randy in his mind and pictures him while silently swooning, *Oh my God, Randy. You are soooo gorgeous!*

Phillip has one more year of high school. *Then, maybe I'll just head straight for Los Angeles where the models in the magazine live. I might even be a model! And maybe Randy will come, too.* He says out loud to himself, "I can dream, can't I?"

Often, when he finishes with his magazines, he lies back, closes his eyes, and conjures up an image of Randy posing for a physique picture. He imagines the scene. *Randy, absolutely beautiful, his nearly naked body in a dance pose, smiling at the camera—at him.* As the feelings well up in him, Phillip buries his face in the pillow and sobs. *He doesn't even know I exist.*

Phillip arrives early for acrobatics at the dance studio. The beginning modern jazz class is underway, so he watches the students from the back of the room. Mr.

Richard, bent over, back bowed up like a cat, is demonstrating a Martha Graham posture and calling out moves to the class at the same time. "Contract! Like a pissed-off cat!" He points to a girl standing close to Phillip. "You too, Blondie. Suck in that gut! Now! Everyone, release. Up straight! Watch me now and do what I do." He does a walking in place pantomime. "Smooth! Get control of those muscles. Go slow. Slower!"

Mr. Richard, as always, dangles a lit cigarette from the corner of his mouth while calling out the steps. He can talk, or even dance while smoking. Phillip doesn't smoke—he tried it two different times, but couldn't get over the choking and, besides, he doesn't like the smell on people's clothes. But Mr. Richard? He looks like Bogart, the cigarette dangling, one eye squinting to avoid the smoke.

Phillip stands at the back, behind the students, and Mr. Richard acknowledges his presence with a glance and a wink. He saunters over to Phillip, eyes locked on his, whispers, "Bonsoir, Phillip." In one smooth gesture, he removes the cigarette from his mouth, kisses the tips of his extended fingers and blows the kiss to Phillip (who giggles). Then, eyes still locked into Phillip's, he calls out to the class, "Pull it in and pose. Belly buttons touching your spine! Jazz hands. Hold!" He pauses, breaking eye contact, puts the cigarette back in his mouth, and looks at the class. "Now release."

Phillip giggles, then modulates his voice for a sultry answer, "Bonsoir, Monsieur Richard." He pronounces "Richard" the French way, without the final "d".

Right now, there is no place on earth that Phillip would rather be. It isn't so much the place, though it is that too. It's the people. And it's the dance, Mr. Richard, everything. He feels safe here. He belongs.

Then Randy walks into the room. He's wearing snug black pants and a short-sleeved black t-shirt, tucked in, showing off his muscular chest and biceps. His hair, light brown with blond streaks (*natural?*), always appears disheveled.

"Oh my God!" Phillip whispers. He loves that Randy dresses plain, but still shows off his body. Randy moves smoothly across the room to greet Mr. Richard—he has an air of confidence that Phillip can't seem to capture for himself.

Randy and Mr. Richard exchange quips, in a whisper. Phillip notices that Mr. Richard is always touching Randy, getting in his face and smiling, flirting.

Lena and her mother arrive just as the modern jazz dance class is breaking up. They stop to talk to Randy and

Mr. Richard, and Phillip hears him ask Randy to stay on and help him spot for their acrobatics class.

Oh my God! This makes Phillip so nervous he retreats to the dressing room. After he changes into his leotards for class, he looks in the mirror, and moves closer to inspect, then pop the pimple on his chin. He uses a pile of paper towels, one after the other, to dry his sweaty palms, but they remain clammy. *I can't go out there!* He goes into the toilet booth and holds his face in his hands. *Oh my God! He's so gorgeous! I'm gonna die!*

He hears the voices of the other students filtering in, so, finally, he flushes the toilet and leaves the dressing room to take his place along the bar. Except for him and Randy, the whole class is female, most of them learning acrobatic moves for cheerleading at one of the high schools in town.

Mr. Richard instructs the class to form a large circle for warm-ups and asks Randy to take over, which he does. Phillip admires his soft-spoken manner—very different from Mr. Richard. Randy stands in the middle of the circle and as he speaks, he turns in a circle, making eye contact with each of the girls.

"Straddle stretches, girls." He flashes a smile at Phillip, which Phillip believes is just for him, and continues, "Get all the way down if you can. If you can't, bounce and hold, bounce and hold until you can."

They continue to warm up with stretches and bends, getting limber and relaxing their muscles. Mr. Richard sidles over to Phillip and asks him to spot with Randy. Phillip tries to be nonchalant, nodding and smiling, "Sure, yes. Sure." *Oh my God!*

When it's time to practice the back flip, or double or triple flips, Randy calls Lena up to demonstrate. Even though she doesn't need it now, they put the safety harness on her and the two spotters hold the tethers at either side so the others can see how it works. Lena prepares by crouching down, then launches into a perfect tucked backflip. Randy narrates while she prepares, in slow motion, another flip, then executes it in a flash. Phillip dutifully pulls the tether tight, matching Randy's hold. Right after this, she surprises the girls by doing a forward flip and a backflip in quick succession, without the guys holding onto the harness. They smile and clap, and she smiles back while unhooking the harness, then takes a deep comical bow and skips off across the studio where Mr. Richard waits.

Phillip can see that at least one of the girls has eyes for Randy and is flirting with him as she steps up to be first to try the back flip. *She's completely taken with him, too.*

After they strap her into the harness, Randy demonstrates the preparation and talks about momentum. Phillip is in rapt attention, admiring how Randy instructs them, how he looks, just everything about him. When Phillip realizes that he has a silly grin on his face, he pinches his lips together, and instinctively tries to cover his mouth with his hand, except that he's holding the harness tether for the girl. *I look so stupid!*

When each girl has had a chance to practice her back flip, Mr. Richard and Lena come back to the circle. He tells everyone to do a walking handstand for 30 seconds, walking around the circle. "Don't run into anyone, and keep your legs hiked straight up." Some do just fine, others lose their balance and have to start over. They do back walkovers, and the class devolves into chatter and laughter. Richard, Lena, and Randy are in conversation across the room.

When Richard dismisses the class, the girls go scampering off to the dressing room, while Phillip stands by himself, feeling very self-conscious. Awkward. He doesn't know if he's now part of the teaching team—Mr. Richard, Randy, Lena, and him? Or not. He would love to talk to Randy, but what about? Not knowing what else to do, Phillip disappears into the men's dressing room again, the only guy there, and changes back into his street clothes.

When he opens the door, he nearly runs into Randy, who is coming in. Randy smiles. Phillip melts.

"Hey, Phillip. Richard is having a party Friday night. He asked me to invite you."

Phillip is nearly speechless. "Me? Are you going? I mean, here? Or where?"

Randy nods his head.

"Sure. Yes. Where? Where he lives?"

"Yes. He lives three doors down to the left. On Harrison. There's a purple door. Upstairs. The only apartment up there. 9:00."

"Sure. Great! Thanks, Randy." He reaches out to touch Randy's arm, but pulls back, thinking he shouldn't.

"See you then."

Phillip is beside himself. *Oh my God!*

Friday, all day, Phillip paces around the house, fretting about what he should wear. He would give anything to talk to his big sister. She was always popular at school, a member of the prom queen's court, and she dated a guy on the basketball team. Now, she's in summer school in Vermont and he's not allowed to make long-distance calls, even to her. Anyway, he could never tell *her* that he's in love with a guy. *But she could help with what to wear, couldn't she, without knowing? And what will I say to Randy?*

Without his sister's advice, Phillip settles on his freshly ironed chinos, a red and white pin-striped shirt, and white bucks. Close to 9:00, he drives downtown to the dime store, parks his car, and walks past the studio. When he sees the purple door, he's too nervous to go inside, so he walks past the door and heads around the block, giving himself a pep talk the whole way. Back at the purple door, he takes a few deep breaths, opens the door, and ascends to the only apartment upstairs. He knocks timidly, half hoping no one will answer, but almost immediately, it swings open and a very strange woman he doesn't know motions for him to come in. He's not even sure he's in the right place, but she bellows, in an unmistakable man's voice, "Why, if it isn't Mr. America in his Pat Boone pin-stripes! You're in the right place, Sugar Buns. Step right in!" She grabs his hand and escorts him in, closing the door behind her. Phillip's face is frozen in a surprised smile. He has no idea what to think.

The apartment is very dimly lit, candles on every surface of what looks to be the living room, and blue light shining from a hallway. Phillip's eyes haven't yet adjusted to the dark, so he can hear but not see people talking. There's a hubbub of people and clinking glasses just beyond what appears to be the kitchen doorway. He hears laughter coming from a distant room, and the place has an unfamiliar pungent odor. He's heard that once you've smelled marijuana, you can detect it anywhere—he wonders if that's what he's smelling. And there's piano music, but no sign of a piano.

He's taking it all in when Mr. Richard comes around the corner. "Brucey-Poo, have you met Phillip? He's one of my lovely dancers."

"We've met, Richard. When he came in, he flashed me those dazzling baby blues!"

Phillip hadn't done that intentionally, but people did sometimes make over his blue eyes and his long, long eye lashes. Mr. Richard takes his hand and leads him past Brucey-Poo into the living room—a living room with no furniture other than bean bags, cushions scattered around the floor, and coffee tables holding candles of every size and shape.

"What are you drinking, dahling?" Mr. Richard asks Phillip, and of course, Phillip hasn't a clue. He's never actually had anything but a few sips of beer, which he didn't like at all.

"I don't know, Mr. Richard. What do you have?"

"Call me Richard, dahling." Again, while locking Phillip's eyes in a seductive gazes, he whispers, "I have whatever your heart desires, my dear, but that's not what you mean, is it?"

Phillip blushes, and with his hand over his mouth, stifles a giggle.

Mr. Richard is louder than usual, and is exaggerating his moves, extending arms, bent at the wrist, calling attention to himself. Turning to Phillip, he gushes, "You'll love a Grasshopper. They're yummy! Brucey'll get you one.

"Brucey-Poo, bring Studley here a Grasshopper."

Grasshopper? Mr. Richard scampers off to the next person coming in the door.

Phillip, eyes now accustomed to the dim light, looks around. He doesn't see anyone he knows, but why would he expect to? Brucey-Poo, his new best friend, delivers a drink—green! He looks at it, brings it closer to his eyes, brow furrowed, and Brucey-Poo simply says, "Crème de Menthe, Studley. Not a real grasshopper, dahling."

Phillip saunters over to the corner of the living room, leans against the wall and takes a pull on the straw. *Grasshopper! Nothing like beer.* He nearly inhales it, all of it. *Wow, minty—I don't feel anything!*

The piano music he's hearing sounds live, so he goes in search of the piano, which takes him into the blue room. Even in the dark, he recognizes the studio piano player who is sitting on a three-legged piano stool, legs crossed, brown cigarillo dangling from her mouth, playing some bluesy songs on a piano that's slightly out of tune. He moves a bit closer, as he's always wanted to do, looks at her fingers on the keyboard (she's oblivious to him). *I wonder how those fingers know exactly where they're supposed to go and when—she never even opens her eyes!*

He notices the strange smell again. It's much stronger here. Suddenly, Mr. Richard is standing beside him.

"Toke?" he offers Phillip what he figures is a lit joint.

Phillip has never been at a party where people are smoking marijuana, but he's heard plenty about it. Some teachers have said that it's the road to heroin addiction and certain death, so he's always been nervous about trying it, but, Mr. Richard isn't a heroin addict, so, sure, he'll try it.

He takes the joint, and draws some smoke, and blows it right back out. *I don't feel anything.*

He hands the joint back to Mr. Richard who's whispering in his ear. "You have to inhale. Take a drag, breathe in, and hold it."

Phillip tries again. Inhales and holds.

Richard watches him. "That's right."

Then he starts coughing, choking, out of control. Now embarrassed, he tries to stifle the cough, but it keeps bursting out. Brucey-Poo hands him another Grasshopper, and he takes a sip. The coughing subsides, but now he does feel funny. Mr. Richard is up close, looking at him with quizzical eyes. "Good shit, huh?"

Phillip starts laughing and makes his way to the corner where he plops down into a luscious beanbag. Now he is mellow and he can't remember what was so funny. He gets comfortable, taking in, even studying, everything and everyone. Then, someone walks by and looks quizzically at him, and it strikes him as funny—very funny. He laughs and laughs and loses track, again, of what's so damn funny, then thinks of the guy again and laughs even harder. He lies back in his bean bag and tries to stop, but gives in to the laughter. When he looks up, he sees Lena.

"Lena? What are you doing here, girl?"

"Me? What are you doing here, Phillip?"

Phillip starts laughing again, and can't quit. Every time he looks at Lena, he starts laughing all over again. He sees someone else he recognizes, but before he can figure out who it is, the two of them disappear.

Someone hands him a joint, again. He obliges and passes it back. Bruce, *sweet Brucey-Poo*, comes by with another drink and a chocolate cupcake. *Oh my God!* He wolfs down the cupcake like he's never going to eat again, sucks back the drink, then lies back in his beanbag and listens to the conversations all around him. For what seems like a really, really long time, he picks random words and phrases from the din: "Beatniks, Ginsburg is one of us." *One of us?* "Burroughs in Mexico City." *Who is us?* "Kerouac and Carr, hell—they're all queer." *What?* "To hell with that…" *What?* "What's going on in San Francisco, baby?" *San Francisco!* and on and on.

Queer? He starts laughing again, and then someone he doesn't know is kneeling down in front of him. "You okay, sweetheart?" He squeezes Phillip's thigh and smiles with questioning eyes.

Before Phillip can answer, Randy appears behind the stranger. "He's okay, Jim. He's a friend of mine. And he's jailbait. I'll take care of him."

"Oh, right-o, Randy, love." Jim disappears.

"Why am I jailbait, Randy?"

"Phillip, you're queer as hell but you're too young, and you need to know what the laws are. They're out there waiting for you and me and everyone here to screw up. Jail is not a pretty place."

Phillip was startled, and suddenly, scared to death.

"C'mon, Phillip, let's shag before the serious stuff comes out." He holds his hand out to Phillip, who reaches for it and starts the tricky task of becoming upright. He's grateful for the help, but what he's thinking about is that he's holding hands with Randy. He tries to wipe the self-satisfied grin off his face, but he's not in control of that either.

The next morning, Phillip wakes up in bed, at home, with a horrific headache and no recollection of how he got there. His stomach feels rocky, and the last thing he remembers is Randy escorting him out of the party. *Oh shit! He must think I'm a drip.* He hears lawn mowers mowing and kids' laughter, but has no inclination to get out of bed.

Then he looks at his alarm clock. *Oops, gotta get up.*

It's Saturday. He's an usher this afternoon at the movie theater. It's a crummy job, but he gets to see all the movies that come here, so it's not too bad. *The Greatest Show on Earth* is premiering today, and he hopes he'll get to see it at least once today.

He's in the kitchen making toast when the phone rings. It appears that he's the only one home, so he gets it. It's Lena.

"Can I come over, Phillip?"

"Sure, why?"

"I'll be right over."

In what seems like two minutes, she was at the door knocking.

"Come on in, Lena! The door isn't locked."

Lena comes in and looks at Phillip, who's wearing the wrinkled version of his Mr. America outfit from last night.

"You look terrible. Hey, you were really wasted."

"Yeah. That was a blast, huh?"

"Look Phillip, promise not to tell anyone who you saw me with last night? Or even that you saw me last night. I never thought anyone I knew would be there. I mean, from school."

Phillip is confused, but he's not saying anything, just nodding and waiting for the rest.

She's pacing now. "We're already in enough trouble. Last Monday, some dumb teacher, I don't know which one, saw me get out of Jerry's car at school and told the principal. When the principal called me into the office and asked about it, I told him exactly what Jerry told me to say—that I had missed my bus and was walking to school when he stopped and gave me a ride."

"Jerry? Jerry who?"

"Mr. Spencer—Jerry. You saw him last night. Remember?"

"Mr. Spencer, the history teacher? Last night? I did?"

"Oh, Phillip. Sometimes you're such a dipstick. You saw us together last night." She's in his face, getting louder and louder. "At the party. You don't remember?"

"Oh, right. What's wrong with him?"

"He's not allowed to go out with me, is what's wrong with him. He's a teacher! And he's twenty-two years old. He could get fired. Or worse. He's afraid they'll put him in jail."

"You're going together? Oh, honey! You? Going with Mr. Spencer? Wow. He's so cool! Are you in love?"

Ignoring his questions, she goes on, "But they can't prove we did anything. I mean, it's not against the law for him to give me a ride, right?"

"Really?"

"For all the principal knows, it was just a ride, right?"

"Sure. What does your mom say?"

"Are you kidding? My mom doesn't know. And mum's the word, Phil. She would kill me, kill us both. Not for him giving me a ride. For us going out. Swear you won't tell anyone! Swear?"

"Sure, Lena. He's a cool cat, Mr. Spencer. But I'm not saying anything. Just—wow!" Changing the subject, "Hey, Lena? Did you see how I got home last night? My car is here, but I don't remember anything."

Lena, hands on her hips, frowns in disapproval, "Randy and his friend—I don't know his name—brought you home. Randy drove your car, and the friend took him back to Mr. Richard's house. You're lucky they were there."

"Yeah, I know."

"So, you don't remember seeing Jerry—Mr. Spencer—and me last night?" Lena glares at Phillip and waits for his answer. He shrugs his shoulders.

"Oh great! I just told you. So now you know. I'll kill you if you tell a soul, Phillip."

Phillip raises both hands, as if to stop her in her tracks. "Hey, you wanna go to the movies this afternoon? *"Greatest Show on Earth?"*

"No. I have to work the concessions tonight. God, I hate that drive-in. The boss wants us to wear short shorts, and then the creeps come into the concession stand and make snide comments. And the boss is even worse. Every time he passes behind me, he touches…"

She steps toward the door. "Promise?" she asks, opening the door.

"Promise." He closes the door and waves goodbye. He butters his toast and pours a cup of coffee, then sits at the kitchen table, slowly digesting what just happened.

Then he thinks about Randy bringing a friend to the party. He's disappointed, but he takes comfort in knowing that he'll see Randy at the dance studio tomorrow.

Maybe, just maybe…

Refuge from the Storm

Doris steps out of her bedroom wearing a beige sundress with clusters of tiny blue forget-me-nots. She's thinking out loud, "Whew! I love a good bath! Don't you, Lacey, honey? I feel better than I have for an age. You must be good medicine for me." She turns to Lacey, who's sitting at the table staring out the window. "Or maybe it's the pills. Haha! Whatever it is, I sure do like it."

She nearly floats to the hall mirror, eyes her figure, turns from one side to the other, looks over her shoulder, and nods her head in approval. She stops her preening to look at Lacey, who is ravenously biting her nails. Her finger tips are angry, almost bloody, though the bruises are just about gone now.

"Come here, Sugar. Let me see those nails." She reaches for Lacey's hands. "Oh my, Lacey, honey. Your fingers are a sight. Right down past the quick! Don't they hurt?"

Lacey pulls her hands away, grimaces apologetically, and nods. She starts a retreat to the kitchen, but then turns to Doris and says, "I've been here almost three days. Do you think they'll find me here and take me back to the trailer?"

"Not on your life, honey. No one's going to take you anywhere. That is, not unless you want to go? I know you must miss your mama, honey, but it doesn't seem like that'd be a good place for you to go now. Come here. Let's see if we can find something to put on your nails that will help keep you from biting them. Okay?"

Harold had called Doris yesterday from Cincinnati and said he was worried that they may have gotten into a *situation* they couldn't handle, with Lacey and all, so he'd made an appointment for her and Lacey to go talk to the minister, Reverend J.B. at the Methodist Church. They're to be at his office today at 2:00. Just to see if he can help Lacey, he'd said. Doris trusts Harold, and when she can, she does whatever he asks of her.

Looking into the hallway mirror, Doris catches Lacey watching her brush her hair. She bends upside down and allows her hair to fall, almost to the floor, then gathers it high on the back of her head and secures it with a rubber band. She chooses a blue ribbon to match the blue in the flowers on her dress, then ties it in a bow around the pony tail. Looking through the mirror at Lacey watching her, their eyes meet and they both break into a grin. *This girl is not a "situation." She's family. Harold just doesn't understand. Yet.*

Doris applies a liberal coat of bright pink lipstick, which she blots several times, leaving her lip imprints, top and bottom, on the Kleenex. She playfully opens the Kleenex to see her lips—holds the big pink Kleenex up to the mirror next to her open mouth. "Look at me, Lace!" They both have a good laugh.

Slipping into her beige sandals, she turns to Lacey, "Okay, honey. Bathroom's all yours. Just push the door to and you'll see a fresh towel on the back of the commode. While you bathe, I'll pick out a nice dress."

Lacey slips into the bathroom, shuts the door. Doris keeps yakking about the dress and shoes she's picked out, even though she can hear the water running in the bath and should know that Lacey can't hear what in the world she's saying.

"I have a sweet white sundress here—let's see, here it is—it's got big ole yellow polka dots. This'll be so pretty on you with your red hair and freckles and all, don't you think?" She didn't wait for an answer. "Hey, good thing we're both about the same size, isn't it? You know, even our shoes are the same size. We must be sisters! So funny. Don't you worry, Lacey, honey, I've got everything you need."

These days, she goes back and forth, one minute, quiet and pensive, the next, exuberant and babbling. This transformation amuses her and she says so out loud to Lacey. "Would you listen to me jabbering on and on? I think I'm getting better, by golly! Ha! Harold will be surprised."

She and Lacey have talked almost non-stop since that first night. Well, mostly Doris talks and Lacey listens. But Doris hasn't mentioned her grandfather again after that first night when she told Lacey what he did to her. When she feels sad and can't bring herself to say anything, she closes her eyes, or she watches as Lacey busies herself with housework—ironing, tidying up. Whatever needs doing. There's always something that Lacey is cleaning or putting straight, which Doris does appreciate, because sometimes she just needs the time to sit and think. And she likes that Lacey doesn't talk out of turn. Sometimes they both just need quiet.

Doris has come to see Lacey as a friend and confidant, even though she is only in high school. She seems older than her years, and Doris reckons that's because she's had to take care of herself. She's had to grow up fast, or die! Doris does worry about what will happen to Lacey when Harold comes home—she knows that Lacey has no safe place to go. Lacey never mentions her mother or what her mother must be thinking, and Doris can only imagine why. Probably that no-good scumbag of a boyfriend has told her lies. She must—she will—protect Lacey. She may be the only one who can understand.

After her bath, Lacey barely cracks the door and asks, "What should I put on, Miss Doris?"

"Oops—I forgot to get… oh honey, just grab my robe on the back of the door."

Doris places the dress she's chosen on her bed as Lacey looks on. She smooths out the wrinkles in the skirt with her hands, then stands back and surveys the dress. She picks a pair of white sandals to go with it, and sets them on the bed next to the dress.

She turns to Lacey and says, "You'll be cute as a bug in this, honey! Go ahead and find some undies—you know where they are—in the dresser over there, and get dressed. I'll be in the living room."

Lacey's eyes refuse to meet Doris's as she steps out of the bedroom in the borrowed dress and sandals, but she stops in front of her, hiding her chewed fingers behind her back.

"Honey, my heavens! You look darling in that dress. It is you! Here. Sit down. Let me fix your hair."

Doris talks while she's brushing Lacey's hair, trying to tame the cowlick on the left side of her part. "Now Lacey, we have to get ourselves to the church and talk to that minister. Harold says he's real nice. And we can't go to the church looking scruffy. You have to respect ministers, even if you don't believe all that stuff they tell you." She moves behind Lacey so they can both look in the mirror, and holds the hairbrush aside as she looks into Lacey's reflection.

Lacey, looking worried, asks, "But what are you going to say to him? About me, I mean."

Doris shrugs her shoulders, "Harold says the reverend will help us figure this thing out."

Lacey's forehead is still wrinkled, "What thing?"

"How we can help you, Lacey, honey. But no one is going to tell anyone our secrets. Yours or mine. We have a pact. Remember? Mostly, we just have to make a plan. I reckon, eventually, your mom's going to want to know what happened and where you are, right? But you don't ever want to go back there, right?"

Lacey watches Doris in the mirror, silently shrugs her shoulders.

Now Doris brushes Lacey's hair with conviction, finally giving up on conquering the cowlick. For the final touch, she finds two hats, a white one with a large brim for Lacey, and a smaller straw hat for herself. Doris puts the hat on Lacey and turns it, just so, making sure that when she looks down, it hides her face.

Doris offers, "There you go! No one will recognize you in this hat."

Lacey looks in the mirror and nods her head in agreement. Doris situates her own hat on her head, and they set out for the church, taking the back way around the block to avoid being seen by the neighbors who might recognize Lacey.

When they open the large carved mahogany front door to the church vestibule, Doris gets the scent of fresh floor polish as it wafts past them and dissipates into the fresh summer breeze. They step into a large room where a machine is running. She watches the janitor, who is barely holding onto the handle of the gigantic floor polisher as it runs in circles, buffing the floor, seemingly on its own. When he gets to the far corner, he flips the switch off, and they watch him shuffle into an adjacent room. In the background, they hear someone playing the piano—it actually sounds more like practicing—stopping in mid-tune, then starting over, again and again.

They proceed up the three stairs following the sign to the minister's office, where his secretary welcomes them and invites them to take a seat to wait for the reverend. Doris isn't exactly sure what to expect next—she and Harold don't go to church much at all. She's met this minister, most recently at the Memorial Day ice cream social, but doubts he'll remember her.

His secretary knocks lightly on his door, then cracks it open to let him know they're here. He comes right out. "Come in, young ladies. I've been expecting you."

Doris marches right up to him and offers her hand and introduces herself. She allows that he probably doesn't remember meeting her, but that they met on Memorial Day at the park. And she liked his talk at the cemetery, she tells him. He nods and says, "Yes, Mrs. Swank, I remember you. Memorial Day. Yes, mmm-hmm." Doris is pleasantly surprised that he remembers her. She introduces Lacey.

He invites them to take a seat and motions to the two chairs in front of his large, highly polished desk. They take their seats but Doris can see that Lacey is nervous, so she scoots her chair close enough that she can touch her if she needs to.

The reverend seats himself behind his desk. He swivels around in his chair, and picks up what looks like a brand new writing pad from a stack on his bookcase, then places it on his desk in front of him. He carefully chooses a pen from a holder filled with different sorts of pencils and pens, then looks up at Doris.

Doris glances at Lacey, who's looking at the assorted framed pictures on the wall of two young girls, a woman, a dog, and a cat. The reverend sees her looking at the pictures and says to her, "These are my twin girls, Sheila and Sharon. They're in fourth grade, or will be in September. Do you know them?"

Lacey shakes her head no, and then changes her mind, nods, "Yes. Well, no. But I've seen them. They're very sweet, and pretty, too."

The reverend smiles and nods in agreement.

Doris pipes up, "Harold and I have twins, too! They're boys though. Going on three years old. Into mischief all the time, they are! They're in Mayfield with their cousins right now." The reverend nods and smiles.

Casting a lingering glance at the pictures, then at each of them, pen in hand, he begins the conversation. "Doris, your Harold called yesterday and seemed very concerned about you. He asked that I talk with you about how this young lady comes to be staying with you, and just what her situation is. I'm sure you know that he's quite worried?"

Doris can feel Lacey shrinking in her chair. Her face is distorted, and she looks at Doris with pleading in her eyes. Doris looks right in her eyes, then, as if pulling a zipper, draws her fingers across her tightly closed lips.

The reverend, watching the unspoken promise, appears keenly aware of the situation. He pushes a box of Kleenex toward the two. Doris pulls a tissue from the box and puts it in Lacey's hands and the reverend jots something on the pad in front of him.

Doris finally speaks. "Yes, Lacey has been staying at our house. She has been helping me, sir. She's a very good worker, and I've been under the weather. She stays with me for now."

The reverend asks again, "Harold seems to think that Lacey is in some sort of trouble. Is that right?"

He looks at the girl. "Do your parents know where you are staying, Lacey?"

Doris asks, "Lacey, honey, do you want me to do the talking, or do you want to do it yourself?"

Lacey shrugs her shoulders and looks at the Reverend. He puts down his pen, and looks into her eyes, "I will not share with anyone, including your parents, what either of you tell me here today. But I do need to know your parents' names and address—it's a matter of ethics. Do you understand?"

Doris takes stock of him while his full attention is on Lacey. When he speaks, it is a soft voice that somehow matches his green (or would you call them hazel?) eyes, expressive and kind, but searching. And she's intrigued with the big dark shadow—his closely shaven beard—on his roundish face. The shadow is glistening—slightly moist with sweat. *He's like a cuddly teddy bear!*

Doris whispers to Lacey, "Honey, it's okay to tell him this much."

Finally, Lacey blurts out, "We live on the Hills Road, in the second trailer. My mother, her name is Sadie Boyles, she works at Sunshine Laundry and Dry Cleaning, but she's not usually home, sir, Reverend."

He writes and then says, "Thank you, Lacey. Is your last name Boyles, too?"

She nods.

"And your father?"

She shrugs her shoulders, cocks her head to one side, and looks directly at him.

"So you don't live with your father?"

Lacey doesn't move, continues to glare at him.

He waits for a moment. "I see... Thank you, Miss Boyles. Now I will want to talk with each of you ladies separately."

Doris looks at him and asks, sharply, "Why? Why can't we stay together?"

"It's a matter of privacy and confidentiality. I need to talk with people one on one—it's easier to make sure no one's privacy is violated. But I want to assure you both, again, that what you tell me remains with me. Do you trust me?"

Both Lacey and Doris look intently at him, and then at each other. Doris nods her head. She knows that most everyone in town thinks he's the nicest man ever, and to her, that means trustworthy. Lacey watches Doris, but says nothing.

He takes charge. "Good. Now, Miss Boyles, may I ask you to wait in the choir room while I speak with Mrs. Swank?"

He opens the door and his secretary motions to Lacey to follow her.

"Okay, Mrs. Swank, shall I call you Doris?"

"You betcha, Reverend."

"So, can you tell me in your own words what has happened that resulted in Miss Boyles staying with you for… how long? Without her mother's permission?"

"Four days. So far. Yes, sir."

As she speaks, he jots down his notes and looks up at her to continue.

Doris feels a knot forming in her stomach. She isn't sure what she can say without breaking her pact with Lacey.

"Sir, I didn't know Lacey until the other night when she came to my house to help me with cleaning and such. I hadn't been feeling well, so Harold hired Rosie to help me. (Rosie right across the street? Do you know her?) So, when Rose came over? She brought Lacey to help. And then, as it happened, Rose had to leave to go home, but she couldn't take Lacey, so I told her to just stay and please help me with dinner. So she did!

"Sir, she was a mess. She had bruises on her wrists, and she had a large, red mark on her face. She had bloody scrapes on her legs, and she was barefoot—didn't even have any shoes. And you could see, Mr. Reverend, she was afraid. Very much afraid. I knew that something bad happened to her."

He sits quite still, looks at Doris and waits for her to continue.

"Sometimes women know certain things—you know? They see certain things that may have happened. I saw that with her. We talked for quite a while about her mother, and it turns out her mom has a boyfriend at home and there's a half-brother there, too, at least one, maybe more. She finally told me what happened to her that afternoon. Sir, Reverend. You can't imagine it."

The reverend leaned forward a bit, "I think I can imagine it, but do go on, Doris."

"Well, sir, this is the part that I promised not to say. I need permission from Lacey." Abruptly, she stands and bolts toward the door.

He cautions, "Doris? It's my job as a counselor to…"

She interrupts, "Wait, Reverend. I promised." She heads out to find Lacey and reappears shortly with her in tow.

When the two women come back into his office, the reverend motions for them to take their seats again and closes the door. He continues to encourage them to talk as he gently nods his head, "Okay, girls. Who shall do the talking now?"

Doris begins by telling him that she recognized right away that Lacey had been hurt by someone, but that she seemed shy, or afraid, or both, to tell what had happened to her earlier that day.

The reverend starts to talk, but Doris raises her hand to stop him. She's now speaking to Lacey, "Lacey, honey, I didn't tell him everything, just about the bruises and cuts. I didn't tell him the rest, but I trust him and I'm going to tell him about my grandfather. Then I think it's okay for you to tell him what happened to you, too. But I won't break our pact, or tell him if you don't want to, okay?"

Lacey nodded and looked down while Doris continued, "Reverend? The reason I could see the signs of what happened to her was because something happened to me when I was just a girl. I've never told anyone, not even Harold, because my mom said it was my fault. I was so ashamed. Then I saw that in Lacey's eyes, the shame, and the bruises and cuts on her arms and legs, and I knew what had happened.

"That's why I told Lacey my story. Because one time, I had no place to go either, and someone helped me. And that's when I promised to look after her. She has nowhere to go, so she is staying at my house. Reverend, no one, not even her mother, has come looking for her! No one."

The reverend nods his head, as if agreeing. "Alright, Mrs. Swank. I understand. Now then, may I ask you to wait in the choir room while I speak with Miss Boyles?"

Lacey searches Doris's eyes for a signal, and Doris says that, yes, she will wait for her outside of his office. She reaches over to touch Lacey's arm, and says, reassuringly, "You can go on ahead and tell him everything, honey. That won't break our pact. It's okay. I'll be right out here when you're finished."

He walks around his desk and opens the door, motioning to his secretary.

Doris smiles and follows the woman to the choir room. She's never been in this part of the church, and is intrigued by the rack of fuchsia robes just inside the room. The woman notices her eyeing them, and says, simply, "Choir robes."

She tells Doris to make herself comfortable, and leaves her in the room. Moments later, she hears a commotion in the hallway and thinks she hears Lacey 's voice. When she hears a door slam, she gets up to check on Lacey.

The secretary looks confused and the Reverend is standing there when Doris rounds the corner.

Doris demands, "Where's Lacey?"

He answers, "She left. She went off the deep end."

"Why? What deep end?"

"What I said is that sometimes girls think something has happened but it actually hasn't. Or, in cases like this, the girl has probably been involved with the same boys she's accusing, and maybe they had a fight, uh, argument. You know…"

His secretary looks horrified, her hand over her mouth.

Doris glares at Reverend J.B., her anger nearly choking her. "I thought you were supposed to help us. I trusted you! No wonder she left. And you'd better not tell anyone Lacey is staying with me, if anyone even cares. If they come and haul her back to that pit, it'll be on you!"

"Mrs. Swank, you don't know how people like this live. You best stay clear of them."

Without another word, she bolts for the front door, opens it, then turns to the secretary and warns, "And you'd better not tell anyone either!"

She leaves through the great front door, allowing it to bang shut behind her and breaks into a run, yelling out, "Lacey! Lacey!"

She sees no one. Half running and half walking, she heads back to her house, the only place she can imagine that Lacey would go. Instead of taking the long way, she takes the road right past all of the neighbor houses, Phillip's, Lena's, and then gets to her house across from Rosie's. She jogs around to the back door, pounding and yelling for Lacey. And just as she is about to give up, Lacey unlocks the door. Much relieved, she pushes the door open and sees Lacey fling herself into a heap on the couch. Her mouth is open as if to scream, but there is no sound.

"I'm here. I'm here, honey." She pulls Lacey up from the couch and holds her, reassuring her that she's safe, that no one is going to take her back there.

Lacey, her eyes filled with tears, her body stiff, whispers, "You said... you said..."

"I know, Lacey. I know. I thought… And I'm so mad I could spit nails. I thought… But you're safe now, honey. We'll figure this out ourselves. Harold will be home tomorrow, and he'll know what to do."

Doris turns on the radio to try to take their minds off of what happened today, and they both listen, or pretend to listen, to a favorite of Doris's—Johnny Dollar, a story about a detective and a woman named Amelia. The whole time Johnny is solving the crime, Doris is thinking about how to solve Lacey's dilemma.

They keep the blinds closed and eat leftover pork and beans for supper, though neither of them is very hungry. They talk about the possibility of going to Mayfield to see the twins, and maybe even bringing them home, but they avoid the topic of the reverend.

When Harold calls, he says he'll be home early tomorrow and that he's taking her out to eat. Doris tells him their meeting with the reverend didn't really help, and he promises that they will talk about it when he gets home.

Harold is standing in the doorway, his eyes riveted on Doris. She knows he hasn't seen her dressed up since the twins were baptized and she's tickled pink! He breaks into a wide grin. "My, my, Dorie, you're a sight for sore eyes!"

She looks into his eyes, smiles, and beckons him to come to her. He glides across the living room to where she is standing, takes her in his arms, and waltzes her around the room, twirling, then stopping to kiss, laughing and hugging. Doris catches a glimpse of Lacey, looking somewhat embarrassed, scooting into the kitchen, wiping the counter, straightening some things.

Soon enough, the three of them sit down at the table to have a talk. They chatter about going to Mayfield, about the twins, about how much Doris misses them. She says she wants to bring them home this weekend—that she believes she can take care of them now, that she always has Lacey to help. Harold's gaze is on the distant trees beyond the backyard.

After a while, he says it might be a good idea for Lacey to meet Doris's brother and their children, too. "Who knows? They have a lot of room. Maybe Mayfield would be a better home for her? Far away from… trouble."

The idea is startling to Doris, but she sees that Lacey is nodding.

Harold says to Doris that they should go slow with the twins. If she needs help, he says, she can always call Rosie to help. And they can always go back to Mayfield if need be.

That night, Doris lies in Harold's arms until he goes to sleep. She feels at peace for the first time since she can remember. She hopes that she'll feel this good tomorrow, and the next day…

When the Bow Breaks

The phone rings, and, as if on cue, Lena dashes to the hallway to pick up before her mother can get to it. Lena turns her back to her mother and covers her smile with her free hand. She listens intently, whispers a few words, and hangs up the receiver.

Back in her room, she executes her plan. "Hey Mom! I'm going to Susie's house—she's having a swimming-slumber party—for the cheerleaders?"

Throwing some things into her overnight bag, she glances up as her mother appears at her bedroom door. She sees Ursula's critical eye, dreads her questions.

"Who was that?"

Turning back to her packing, Lena answers nonchalantly, "Karen. Why?"

She can feel her face and ears flush and hopes her mother doesn't notice.

"Quite a smile for Karen. What did she want?"

"I'm going to ride with her to Susie's, is all."

"Swimming? At night? You'll need a towel then, huh?"

Lena pushes her way past. "It's okay, Ma. I can't go swimming anyway. 'My friend' is visiting. I'm walking over to Karen's house so I can ride with her to Susie's. I have to hurry. She's waiting for me."

"Alright then. What time will you be home?"

"I don't know, Ma. Afternoon sometime. Don't worry."

"Okay, Lena. Have fun but mind your manners. Susie's parents have a really nice home with the swimming pool and all. They must have a lot of money, huh? We don't want them to think we're just a bunch of Bohunks, do we?" She giggles and slaps her ample rear as she always does when calling herself a Bohunk.

Lena looks away with a scowl, remembering how embarrassed she was when her mother said that in front of Mr. Richard. Opening the front door, she turns back to Ursula. "Don't worry, okay?"

As she hightails it for the corner, gravel crunching under her steps, she feels her mother's eyes piercing the back of her head. She glances back, and, sure enough, Ursula is still standing on the porch, hand on her hip, watching her. Lena stops, whirls around, and flips her fingers in a shooing motion, saying between clenched teeth, "Stop watching me!"

Finally, the stalemate is broken and her mother turns to go back into the house, letting the screen door slam after her. Lena, hands splayed and arms outstretched, pleads to a now empty street, "Leave me alone!"

She makes her way down the road toward the bus stop where, out of sight of her mother, she waits for him.

Lena works at the Springdale Drive-In Movie Theater out on the highway four nights a week except when she has a dance performance. Jerry comes to the movies, usually after the show starts, and parks on the far side where he isn't likely to be recognized, and she joins him after her concession stand intermission shift is over. They've been meeting at the Drive-In two or three times a week since it opened in May until just three weeks ago when he left town to spend time with his parents in Cleveland. She realizes her mother would die if she knew, but she can't help it. They are in love. He says they'll get married when she graduates.

Today, he is back in town and he's picking her up at the highway bus stop, dangerously close to her house. Lena recognizes his red Chevy Coupe from a long way off. She blinks away tears as she watches his approach, feels her heart beating almost out of her chest. She doesn't know how she's going to tell him, but first, she just wants to be with him.

He pulls over, yells over the souped-up muffler noise, "Hi, gorgeous! Hop in! Lord, kitten, I've missed you!"

She climbs in, shuts the door, and slides over on the seat to be close to him. He glances to one side, then the other, making sure no one has seen them, then she turns her face toward him and closes her eyes, her signal for him to plant a kiss on her lips, which he does. Then he puts his arm around her shoulders, like he always does, and pulls her close. When they're driving, she shifts gears for him so he can keep his arm around her. He likes it that way, and so does she.

She leans in, looking coy, and says, "I have a surprise, honey."

He looks at her, smiles, then looks back at the road.

She waits for him to ask and when he doesn't, she continues, "I'm sprung for the night! Mom thinks I'm at Susie's for a slumber party, so I don't have to go home until tomorrow morning."

He keeps his eyes on the road. "Really? You've got to be careful with that. Your mom finds out and my ass is grass!"

Lena responds quickly, "Oh, she won't. Find out, I mean."

He's often told her that he's playing with fire. He knows if anyone sees them together or finds out about them, he'll lose his teaching job. They already had a close call when another teacher saw her get out of his car. And that was when they first started dating. They had a good story for that one, but he sure doesn't want a repeat performance.

He breaks the silence. "Okay. So what do you want to do? We can't go to my place—you know that. We'd be seen."

Lena, no longer smiling, asks, "Can we just go to a motel? Tell them we're married?"

"Uh... Let's just drive and let me think about it. Actually, I'm so hungry, I can't think straight. Aren't you?"

Lena stares straight ahead. All she sees are cornfields, and an occasional Little Miss Sunbeam billboard, but she's not thinking about eating. In fact, she feels more like throwing up.

She sniffles. "I thought you'd be happy."

"I am, darlin'! But I want to get out of town. You know the problem. C'mon. Let's stop by the D. Q. and get some chili dogs. What do you say?"

She squeezes his hand, but doesn't answer. She is preoccupied by her nagging, upset stomach. She knows what that means. She and all of her friends—they all know the signs.

He steals a look at Lena. "What's wrong Princess?"

"Nothing, Jerry. I just missed you so much!" She didn't look at him.

"Well, I can fix that, young lady. I'm going to take you to our place by the lake, as soon as we get something to eat, then we'll figure out the rest. Okay?"

Lena looks up at him and nods. She wonders, *Can he tell?* She is sure though that everything will be okay, now that he's home.

On the radio, Joe Stafford is singing "You Belong to Me"—their song. Lena had proclaimed it so on the two-week anniversary of their first time. She turns up the volume and hums along. Her left hand is absentmindedly stroking his leg and he is pulling her close. It couldn't be better! She loves him because he's strong and so beautiful, and he will protect her. She wants to be in his arms forever.

Their hideaway was a mostly unpopulated, over-grown park where they first did it, which was right after the

Memorial Day parade. Lena had managed to lie her way out of telling her mother where she had been and with whom. Since then, between her friends, her cheerleading practice, and what with her job, they have made many opportunities to be together—most often in the back row of the drive-in movies, always in the car.

Now in their secret place, Jerry, as always, helps her climb into the backseat, then slides in after her, locking both doors. Sure that they're alone, he pulls Lena onto his lap, "C'mere you! It's been way too long! Here, let me help you out of those things."

Usually, he takes his time, kissing her all over before they do it, but tonight he's in a hurry, and it doesn't take him long. She wishes she could have the same feeling he has when they're doing it. *Maybe girls just don't?*

He rests against the back seat and pulls her toward him so she's lying with her head on his chest. He says he loves to look at her, and can't wait until they are in a place of their own where he can watch her dance, naked. When he says that, his eyebrows flicker like Groucho Marx's and he winks at her. She loves it when he does that.

As usual, after they make love, she asks, "Do you still love me?"

He always says, "Of course. Why? Why wouldn't I?" Tonight, though, his eyes are still closed and she hears his breath become slow and rhythmic. It's comforting for her to know that he can sleep with her resting against him.

Out of nowhere, she hears a car making its way down the gravel road. A car door shuts and she hears footsteps on the gravel, coming toward the car. She grabs Jerry and whispers, "Someone's here!"

He responds quickly. In one move, he pushes her and her clothes down behind the seat to the floorboard, and follows, pulling on his pants while scrunched down on top of her. A beam of light illuminates the front seat, bouncing back and forth several times from door to door as they lie in absolute silence. Lena smells the dirt, the remains of the chili dog wrappings, and the sweat on Jerry—she thinks she may throw up right there.

As quickly as he—whoever he is—appeared, he walks away, leaving them scrunched down on the floor behind the front seat. They stay quiet for what seems like an hour. She tries to whisper that she may be sick, but nothing comes out. Finally, the intruder's car door slams, the engine starts and she hears the gravel under the wheels as the car recedes. Jerry sits up and peeks out the rear window. "All clear," he whispers as the tail lights recede on the only road into and out of the park. Finally, she hears only the silence of the park.

Still cautious, he whispers, "I'm going to take a little walk down by the water. If he comes back, duck back down and I'll handle him. Whoever he is, I don't want him to see us together."

Without a word, Lena pulls on her clothes and sits up in the back seat. She pushes the passenger seatback forward, and opens the door to get some air. She says to herself, over and over, *Don't throw up!*

When Jerry comes back to the car, Lena scrambles into the front seat. He instructs, "You can ride up here, but you'll have to duck down so no one sees you in the car."

Feeling a bit better, she lies across the front seat, her head resting in his lap looking at the bottom of his chin. She loves the strength of his chin, the shadow of his beard, his Adam's apple. They drive like this for twenty minutes or so, in utter quiet, until he turns sharply onto a gravel drive. She lifts her head to peek out the side window. Aloha Motel.

"I'm going to go in and check in. I'm not mentioning you, so stay put. Stay down."

Inside the motel room, Jerry immediately closes the blinds. Feeling awkward, Lena plops down on the bed while he fiddles with the TV. "I wonder how this darn thing works. Nothing coming in but snow."

Lena begins talking, picking up where she had left off. "Do you still love me, Jerry?"

"Why are you asking me that now?" He continues to turn knobs and adjust the TV antenna, turns up the volume, but still gets nothing but snow and static. "Damn this thing!"

She ignores his outburst. "Because the only time you say it is when we're doing it, and you didn't say it tonight."

He turns toward her. "Okay—sorry. Sure. I guess I forgot because I got interrupted by the spotlight spy."

"No, I mean, really love me?"

"Sure. I said so."

"Forever? Are we going to get married?"

"What? Not right now. You know that. Why?"

Lena takes some time to smooth her shirt, lies down with her head resting on the pillow, her palms rest on her belly. "Jerry, I have something to tell you."

"I know, I know. You love me." He continues to monkey with the TV channel selector.

"Yes. But that's not what I….. "

Her voice breaks, and the tears start to flow. "That's not what I need to tell you."

"What then? For Christ sake. What? Did someone find out about us?" He reaches for the knob and turns the TV off, but he does not move toward her. "What are you bawling about?"

"I missed my… you know… "

He interrupts, his voice louder. "What? Your what?"

She speaks between sobs, "I'm… late."

"For what? Late for what?" There's a long pause and he sees her hand on her belly. Then, almost whispering, "You don't mean your period, do you?"

She looks at him, nods.

Now Jerry is silent, his face stone cold. He looks at her and then looks away.

She sits up, covers her face with her hands, repeating, "I'm sorry, Jerry! I'm sorry!'"

"Jesus, Lena. How the hell did this happen?" He's pacing back and forth at the foot of the bed with his hand on his forehead. "I used a rubber almost every time! And that one time you said you were okay. Are you… sure?"

She sobs, "No, I don't know for sure. I've never done this before."

"How late?"

With every question, she cries harder, "Five weeks." Now she is sobbing uncontrollably.

"You missed it twice?" He looks at her, then strokes his forehead and begins pacing. "Okay, okay. Take it easy. We'll take care of this." He moves toward her, pulling her forward by her shoulders, forcing her to look him in the eye. "Have you told anyone else?"

She shakes her head no.

"Okay. Don't say anything to anyone, okay? No one. Promise me."

She nods and whispers, "I promise."

He lets go of her, sits down on the bed, hands covering his face.

Lena, still sobbing, reaches to him for comfort but he doesn't respond.

"Hold me! Please, Jerry!" She sobs and wipes her nose with the back of her hand.

He puts his arm around her, but she feels a stiffness in his body that she hasn't felt before.

"Okay, listen. We'll deal with this in the morning."

"What are we going to do?"

"I don't know, Lena. But what we aren't going to do is tell people. We do that and I lose my job and have to go somewhere else to work."

He stands and begins pacing and wringing his hands. "I have some friends in Cleveland that I can talk to tomorrow. But tonight, nothing."

"Cleveland? For what?"

"Look. I need a drink. I'm going to go down to the Starlite. I'll be back. Don't let anyone in."

"You can't leave me!" She bounds out of bed. "Take me with you! Please! I'll stay in the car, please!" She grabs his arm and pulls him away from the door. "Please, Jerry! Pleeeease!"

He tries to shake her loose but she hangs on, sobs and moans, and when that doesn't work, she turns up the volume. She emits a wailing, keening tone and his face turns to rage.

Now *he* is shouting, "What are you trying to do? Damnit, Lena! Stop it! They'll call the police! After what you've dropped on me, I'm the one who should be crying!" He pushes her back on the bed, speaks in an angry but measured tone, enunciating each word, "I'm going to have a drink. You are staying here."

As Jerry turns toward the door, Lena, again, jumps off the bed, grabs his arm and again shrieks, "No! No! Don't leave me! Don't go, Jerry! No!"

Jerry whirls around and pushes her out of the way. She goes limp, falling to the floor and then clutches his leg, letting him drag her as he hobbles toward the door. He finally reaches down, pulls her upright and shoves her toward the bed.

Again, she crumbles into a heap on the floor next to the bed, sobbing and protesting, "Don't go! Jerry! Please!" She stretches her arms out to him, "What about me?"

"You? You did this on purpose, didn't you?" His eyes narrow and he bends toward her. "You don't care if you ruin my life, do you? How do I even know it's mine? How do I even know there is..."

"This isn't my fault!" She sobs and pounds the floor with her fists. "You can't do this to me, Jerry. What am I going to do?"

He turns to the door, grabs the handle.

"I hate you, Jerry! I hate you, I hate you!" Seeing him open the door, she wraps her arms around herself and rocks back and forth, eyes closed. "Please don't go...Jer...ry... pleeeese!"

He is out the door, slamming it behind him. She waits a moment, looking toward the door as though waiting for him to come back, then rises and stumbles to the door. She opens it in time to see him gun his car out of the parking lot, leaving behind a cloud of dust, his tail lights disappearing into the night.

She calls out to the empty parking lot, "Why are you doing this to me? What is happening? I can't believe this!" She begins to feel conspicuous standing there alone, and retreats to the room, closing and locking the door. She sits on the bed, head in hands for the longest time, then she picks up the telephone and dials Phillip's number.

He answers on the fourth ring, "Hello? This is…"

Lena cuts him off, "Phillip? Come get me!" She bursts into tears.

"Why? What's wrong? Where are you? What time is it?"

She sobs, "I'm at the Aloha Motel out on the highway. Come get me!"

"Where? The Aloha? Why?"

She shouts, "Please! Just come!"

"Okay, okay. Wait a minute."

Lena hears muffled sounds as he talks to someone, then he comes back, "I'll be right there. Are you alone?"

"Yes. Hurry, Phillip! Please hurry!"

"Okay, okay. You're alone? How did you get there?"

"Room 7. Just come!"

"Okay. Be there in a jiff."

She listens for the click and dial tone, then drops the receiver into its cradle. She stands at the window, peeking out of a missing slat in the Venetian blinds, watching for Phillip or maybe Jerry.

She wonders what Jerry will do when he comes back and she's not here. *He'll be sorry!* Sure, he didn't plan on this, but neither did she. She was so sure he'd be happy about the baby. He loves her. He said so. She thought he'd marry her for certain, and no one would blame her or him for falling in love!

Phillip's car drives up and he taps the horn. She dashes out the door and hops into the front seat, "Oh, Phil! I'm so confused!"

"What's going on, Lena? What the hey? What are you doing here?"

She makes sniffling noises and in one breath, blurts out, "Jerry brought me here because I told Mom that Susie was having a slumber party and he's been out of town but he's back today and so he picked me up at the bus stop." She sobs, "And we went out to the lake and then we came here and then he went to Starlite's."

"Wait, wait. So why..."

She interrupts, "I'll tell you on the way. Let's get out of here!"

"Wait. Does he know I'm picking you up?"

"No. He was gone when I called you. He left me here. Alone. Let's just go!"

"To where?"

"I have to figure out what I'm going to do, Phillip. I can't tell my parents. They will kill me. They really will. Let's just go."

"To where, Lena?"

"Mr. Richard's apartment. He'll give me a place to sleep."

"We can't just leave with Jerry coming back here wondering what happened to you, can we?"

"Oh, yes we can. Go! Just go, Phillip. I don't want to see him."

"Ok. But…"

Phillip checks the review mirror, then puts his car into reverse and slowly backs out of the parking spot. He heads down the road back to town, Lena looking intently at the cars they are meeting.

He asks again, "So, what happened, Lena?"

Lena sits with her hand over her mouth, shakes her head no. She doesn't answer. Still spinning from what has just happened, she doesn't break the silence until they get to Mr. Richard's apartment. She is relieved to see a light on and says to Phillip, "I'll be fine. Just let me out here."

Mr. Richard answers her knock. His questioning eyebrows reveal deep creases on his forehead and around his eyes, his mouth. His pursed lips hold a smoldering cigarette, which he plucks from his mouth. "Lena? What the hell are you doing here?"

"Can I come in?" She offers no explanation.

He stands aside and nods. Behind her comes Phillip, who Mr. Richard unquestioningly motions in. He looks first at her, then to Phillip. "Hello, sweetheart." Turning to Lena, "Are you bringing me a present?"

She ignores the question and announces, "I need a place to sleep. I've been kicked out of my house."

Phillip spins around and looking directly at her, says, "That's the first I heard that! I picked you up from a motel where you said Jerry took you. What gives, Lena?"

Lena glares at him, trying to hold back tears, "He broke up with me. Jerry. You met him, Richard. The teacher. At your party."

Richard answers with a smirk, "Oh well, dumped! We've all been there. You'll get over it. How about you, Phil-Darlin'? Ever been dumped?"

Phillip shakes his head. "Not really."

Lena interrupts, "I'll never get over it. I'm going to have a baby. He's the father. But I'm not sure. I told him, then he left me at the motel."

"What? You're not sure you're pregnant or not sure it's his? And what's your involvement, Phillip?"

"She called me for a ride. That's all I knew." He looks at Lena. "Oh, my God, Lena. What are you going to do? Your parents! You'll have to get married." He looks at Mr. Richard while she covers her face with her hands and starts crying again.

Mr. Richard, clearly angry, rants, "You're my star. I've put all of my hopes, my studio, all my dreams in you. How could you do this? You're sixteen! Don't you know anything?" He continues to rant. "Well, I'll tell you Lena. This ain't happening. No getting married here. I know people. I'm telling you, this ain't happening!" He storms off and reappears with a pillow and a blanket which he throws on the couch, and tells her to go to sleep.

He looks at Phillip and says, "Either you leave or come sleep with me. I could use…."

Phillip giggles, almost chokes. He makes a bee-line for the door, then Mr. Richard yells after him, "Not a word of this to anyone!"

Lena is looking on in disbelief. She cannot grasp how wrong this has gone, how different from what she had imagined. She wishes now she hadn't left the motel, that she had waited for Jerry. Maybe he would have changed his mind. Maybe he still will.

Mr. Richard is still pacing the floor, but now he is quiet, calculating. Finally, he stops, says to Lena, "What does he say? The creep who got you pregnant?"

"He says I've ruined his life. He says we can't get married. He says not to tell anyone. Not anyone!"

"Okay. Tell him to call me. I know people. Right here. You don't have to go through this—having a kid and ruining your life. We can end this right now. You'll be dancing again in no time."

Lena is stunned. She looks at him, tries to understand what he means.

"Abortion, Lena. It's called abortion. It's called getting rid of this mess before anyone knows. That's what has to happen. I'll take you home in the morning, but I don't want you to talk to your parents about this, hear? I'll make the arrangements, and Mr. Wonderful will pay for it. He won't marry you, if that's what you're thinking. And I doubt he knows anyone who will take care of this for us. So, you either wreck your body and spend nine months somewhere—never dance again—or you trust me to take care of this."

She looks at him, unable to speak. Everything is a blur.

"Do you understand?"

She nods.

He passes through the kitchen, picks up a half-full bottle of something she can't determine, opens it, throws the cap across the room, then takes a long swig. He marches off to his bedroom, turning off the lights as he goes.

She lies back, hand on her belly. Between sobs, she hums, then sings in a whisper, "When the bow breaks…the cradle will fall…down will come baby…"

Shame!

Ursula is piddling around in the kitchen, wondering when Lena is coming home when she hears a car pull up. She hurries to the front window and peeks out of the Venetian blinds expecting to see Karen's parents bringing her home. *Geez Louise! Why in the world is Phillip bringing my daughter home from a slumber party?*

Ursula steps out on the front stoop, hands on hips, as Lena comes up the walk. "What's Phillip doing bringing you home?"

Lena steps up on the stoop, just short of her mother's face, and bellows, "Can't I come or go without you peering out the window or standing on the porch watching my every move? My friends' moms don't do this! Why do you care? It's my life, not yours!"

Ursula takes a deep breath and steps back, "Criminy sakes, Lena! You look terrible. Look at your hair! You look like you slept in your clothes." She loses her composure and grabs Lena's shoulders. "You ask, why do I care? I care because I am your mother! And your dad? If he saw you get out of a boy's car after an overnight stay with girlfriends, he would be in a rage!"

Lena pushes past Ursula, heads straight into her room, slams the door, and shouts at Ursula, "Leave. Me. Alone!"

Ursula hears her sobbing, and now feels guilty for upsetting her. *But it's true—I've never seen Lena go anywhere with no makeup. And even with the curse, she doesn't usually scream and cry.*

Ursula shuts the front door, sits down in her favorite chair, stares at Lena's dance recital pictures covering the wall, wishes she knew whatever it is that's going on with her girl.

She jumps up when the phone rings, and at the same moment, Lena bursts from her room, obviously in a race with Ursula to get to it first. Ursula steps around the corner into the kitchen, and stops just out of sight of Lena, listening to her one-sided conversation. All she hears is a series of yeses and noes. *It sure doesn't sound like a conversation with a girlfriend.*

Ursula can't help herself. "Who was that?"

Lena glares at her, eyes red and cheeks flushed, "As you always say, Mom, 'None of your beeswax!'"

Lena pivots on one foot and marches off to her bedroom, again slamming the door behind her.

Ursula leans on the kitchen sink, looks out the window at Happy, her dead son's old Cocker Spaniel. He's stretched out to the end of his chain, straining to reach something she can't quite see. *Like me, stretched to the end of his rope.*

Boy, was my mother ever right! She said to me when Lena was born that raising a girl was going to be very different from raising the boys.

Lena's bedroom door opens and closes, then the bathroom door slams and locks, jolting Ursula from her thoughts. She is tempted to look in Lena's room to see if there are any clues as to what's going on, but she doesn't want Lena to find her snooping.

Still, I could just wait until the water is running and take a quick look. Probably nothing to find. But after all, I am her mother. I have a right to know, don't I?

When the bath water starts running, she tiptoes to Lena's door, carefully opens it, and sees Lena's purse on the foot of her bed. She picks it up and opens it. Lying right on top, in plain sight, is what appears to be a receipt. She pulls it out and reads across the top "Aloha Motel" and scrawled across the bottom "Cash $15.00 room 7." Ursula emits an involuntary "What?" then freezes. *A motel receipt?*

No longer concerned about being discovered, she bellows as she darts to the bathroom door, "Lena? Lena? What is this? Why do you have a motel receipt in your purse? Is this from last night? This is the slumber party? Tell me you weren't at a motel last night. With Phillip? Lena! Oh my God. Your father. Oh my God!"

Nothing from Lena. Ursula tries the door. Locked. Now pounding with her fist, she shrieks, "Lena! Lena! Open this door!" Clutching the receipt, she makes her way to the living room and sinks onto the couch.

Lena, who has been quiet through this storm, yanks the door open and shouts at Ursula, "How dare you! That was private!"

Ursula, enunciating each word, "Get. In. Here. Now!"

Lena, still clasping a towel around her body, turns to her mother, "I'm getting dressed. You'll have to wait."

Ursula, now in a rage, stands—then lurches across the room, seizes Lena's arm, and yanks her into the living room. "Young lady, I am still your mother and you are still in my house! Stand here!"

Lena jerks her arm away as her towel drops to the floor. She picks it up and clutches it in front of her naked body, still glaring at her mother.

Ursula, her voice shaking, asks, "Where were you last night?"

"Susie's."

"You're lying. Give me her phone number. Now."

"I don't have it."

"Fine. I'll call Phillip. I have his number, you..."

Lena interrupts, "A bunch of us decided to get a motel room and invite our boyfriends to come too. Susie told her parents that we were going to Karen's house, and Angela drove us to the Aloha. But none of the boys ever came. I swear. That's the truth. I called Phillip in the morning and asked him to bring me home."

"How could you do this to me? What will the other mothers think? Do they know you were at a motel?"

"No."

The doorbell rings. Lena, pulling the towel around her, makes a beeline for her room, and Ursula goes to answer the door, warning Lena, "We're not finished, young lady."

Ursula opens the front door to find Betsy, her Avon lady, on the porch, "Hello, Ursula! Is this a good time to show you our new fragrance line?"

Ursula, trying to shift gears, hesitates, not wanting Betsy to feel unwelcome. After a moment, she replies, "Oh sure. Come on in!"

"It's okay if this isn't a good time…"

"No, no, it's fine, Betsy. Come on in."

Betsy is one of her favorite people. She always has a smile on her face and a very pleasant demeanor—even if Ursula doesn't buy anything. Though she usually does. Just because.

Betsy, with her satchel of product samples, follows Ursula to the kitchen table. She opens her case and makes small talk as she pulls out several new fragrances and other items to sample. She always wears one of the new colognes on her wrists so she can give her customers a sniff. Ursula has trouble keeping her mind on the conversation, but is polite to Betsy—and always is to the Fuller Brush man, too—because they're good people, and besides, they have things she can't get anywhere else. And too, when they come, they break up her day.

As they are dabbing and smelling colognes and creams, Lena emerges, dressed, and announces that she's going to see Phillip. Ursula is on her feet, following Lena to the door, and whispers, "You stay here, young lady. We need to finish our conversation."

Lena replies that she will be right back, and leaves, allowing the screen door to slam as she flits down the steps.

Ursula, hands on her hips, stands gaping at her as she walks down the street and turns the corner onto Phillip's street.

Betsy, watching this drama unfold and sensing the tension, comments, "My. She's nearly grown up, isn't she?"

"Yes, Betsy, she is."

Ursula wipes at a tear that is running down her cheek, "Raising girls, you know?"

"Oh, you bet I do. Listen. Do you want me to come back next week? I'm happy to."

"Yes, okay. That would be better. Thanks so much, Betsy." Now her tears are flowing.

Betsy quickly packs up her supplies, but leaves some samples behind. At the door, she turns to Ursula, "Oh, Ursula, I just want to say that everyone so admires you for what you did last Memorial Day. It must have taken so much courage to come out and put the flowers on Norman's grave. In front of everyone. They all talked about that. Everyone is so sorry about your son."

"Oh. Okay. Thanks, Betsy. Thanks."

It's the last thing in the world Ursula wants to hear right now. *Yes, it was easier to raise the boys. Except only boys get killed in action.*

Forcing a smile and waving goodbye to Betsy, she looks across the way toward Phillip's house. No sign of Lena. When Betsy is inside the neighbor's house, Ursula heads out to Phillip's house, walking with a purpose, but when she gets to the corner, she realizes that she doesn't know who else might be there or what she will say. She stops, thinks for a moment, then turns around and rushes back to her house. Once inside, she takes some time to catch her breath, to think about what she will say. She leans on the wall close to the telephone stand and picks up the receiver, cradling it on her shoulder, thinking about him and Lena. *He's always been a really nice boy, trustworthy. Never had reason to doubt him. Lena rides to dance rehearsals and school functions with him all the time. They've always been just friends. Why would he be involved in the girls' slumber party at a motel?*

She phones Phillip.

Phillip answers, "Hello?"

"Hello, Phillip? Is Lena there?"

"Sure. I'll get her."

"Wait, wait. Phillip, can you tell me who else was at the motel where you picked up Lena?"

"Uh, I don't know."

"Was there a boy there with her?"

"No."

"Were the other girls there?"

"No. I don't think so?"

"Phillip, when I tell Jon that you brought Lena home from a motel, he will rip your head off. Do you understand?"

"It wasn't me! It was Mr. Spencer. She called me to come get her because he left her at the motel by herself. Last night. I took her to Mr. Richard's apartment downtown, which is where she wanted to go, and then picked her up this morning. She asked me to. What was I supposed to do when she called me?"

Ursula hears Lena shrieking in the background, "Don't tell her! Phillip!"

Ursula explodes, "What? Mr. Spencer? The teacher? Left her at a motel? Is that what you're telling me? Phillip?"

"Yes."

"My God, Phillip. Now I've heard it all! I can't stand it! Tell her I said to get over here right now. And you need to come, too. If I have to call her dad at work, it won't be pretty."

"Just a minute, okay?"

There is a pause, she hears muffled conversation, then, "We'll be right there."

"I'll be watching."

She hangs up the phone and begins pacing to the front door and back again. When Lena and Phillip come up the walk, Ursula is holding the door open. She follows them in and motions for them to sit at the table.

She stops and turns to Lena, and in a measured cadence, says, "I want you, young lady, to tell me right now exactly what you did, where you went last night, and who you were with."

Lena stares at her mother, lips pursed and jaw clenched. Phillip stares at Lena, and Ursula leans against the sink, arms crossed, staring back at Lena. Her eyes still fixed on Lena, she says, "Okay, then. Phillip? Why don't you tell me how you came to be at a motel with my daughter?"

Phillip shifts his eyes to Ursula, shaking his head vigorously while denying Ursula's accusation, "No, ma'am. I wasn't at the motel. Lena called me and asked me to pick her up. I did. What could I do? She made me swear not to tell you. And like I said…"

Lena jumps in, "I did not! I just needed a ride."

She and Phillip exchange scowls.

Ursula shakes her head violently. "Don't lie to me, young lady! No one believes you anymore."

She moves toward the table, her eyes piercing Lena's, and with her finger jabbing the air toward Lena's chest, says, "This is not about Phillip! You are the one who told me you were going to a slumber party at Susie's. A lie!"

She continues, almost screaming, "Why were you at the Aloha Motel? Who took you there?"

Silence. Lena looks down at her hands, clasped on the table in front of her, offers nothing.

Ursula looks at Phillip. "Who did you say took her there?

Phillip, looks at Lena and answers in a matter-of-fact voice, "Mr. Spencer. From school. Our history teacher. She told me he took her to the motel and left her there. That's why she called me."

Ursula is confused. "You said that before—I don't understand, Phillip. How did he get involved?"

To Lena, Ursula asks, "Why on earth did Phillip take you to Mr. Richard's last night? To the dance studio? What about the slumber party? Who else was at the motel?"

Lena stares at the table, and barely audible, says, "No one. There was no slumber party."

Ursula, screaming, "You lied to me? You lied! You were with your teacher? Why? Why were you with him?"

Lena, still sitting, stares at the table while Phillip has backed away toward the living room.

Lena blurts out, "I love him. He loves me, too. That's what! I love him!" She buries her face in her hands, sobs. Then whimpers, "I… love… him, Mommy."

Ursula, now reeling, continues, "Are you kidding me? Well, this is a shameful thing you've done. No wonder he left. Any man will leave once he gets what he's after. What did you expect?"

Ursula offers no sympathy, clutches her hands against her chest. She turns her back on Lena, stares out the kitchen window.

Phillip moves a step toward Lena, and quietly urges, "Tell her, Lena. You have to."

Ursula spins around and staggers to the table, bracing herself. "There's more? What? What more?"

Lena continues to whimper, head in hands.

Ursula looks at her, shakes her head. "Don't tell me you're in trouble? Not that too!"

Lena slowly pulls her head up, but still not looking at her mother, says in a child-like voice, "He told me he loved me. That we'd get married."

"Look at me, Lena. Look at me! How could you be? You have the curse…oh…"

Her hand over her mouth, Ursula realizes she has just said something that should never be uttered in mixed company.

Lena ignores her question. "When I told him—told him I'm late—way late, he was angry! Then he left me at the motel by myself. All alone! What am I going to do, Mommy?"

Phillip comes to her rescue. Putting his arm around her shoulders, he explains, "He wasn't anywhere in sight when I got there, so Lena asked me to take her to Mr. Richard's, because she couldn't come... well, you know. She didn't want you to know. She was really upset. She just needed a ride."

Her arms flailing, Ursula shouts, "And you couldn't call me? What did you expect from him?"

Lena looks her in the eye and cries out, "He loves me. I thought we would get married. He said we would."

"Oh, uh-huh. Well, I guess you'd better call him, then—Mr. Teacher—and tell him to get his fancy-pants self over here right now or face the law!"

Lena, looking frightened, interjects, "Jerry. His name is Jerry Spencer. What law?"

Ursula continues, "It's called statutory rape. That's what happens when a grown man gets a high school girl pregnant. There, I said it. Pregnant. That's right, isn't it?"

"No, Mom, no! He didn't rape... He called earlier to see if I was alright. He asked me not to tell anyone."

"Well, you can tell him the cat's out of the bag! And he'll marry you or..."

Ursula turns to Phillip. "You're a decent young man, Phillip. I'm sure you wouldn't take advantage of a young girl like he has."

"No, ma'am."

"You need to go on home now. And you don't need to go telling anyone about this, you hear? I expect they'll all know soon enough, but you don't need to tell them."

"I won't. But Mr. Richard says he can get this fixed so Lena's life isn't ruined."

"He knows too? Good God! Her dance coach, you, and who else?"

She looks at Lena, "Why don't you just put it on the front page of the *Times-Union*?

Ursula wonders aloud, "How will I ever face people in this town again?"

Phillip slips out the front door and, without a word, sprints down the front steps. He wastes no time getting to his street corner. Ursula watches as he rounds the corner toward his house.

Shaken by this news, Ursula eases into her favorite living room chair, her body rigid. She studies the pictures on the wall as though she's never seen them before. Lena moves toward the doorway, but Ursula stretches her arm in front of her, hand signaling her to stop. She orders Lena, "Sit down."

Ursula is calm now. She studies the pictures and begins to ramble. "It isn't as though I never imagined this could happen to you. But I didn't think it would be so soon or in this way. You're so young." She pauses for a long moment, looks at Lena. "And, you know? I often remind your Dad, 'Our Lena? She's a smart girl. She knows how much we sacrifice to give her lessons and all the best things—the costumes, the clothes, the hours and hours spent downtown, the dazzling shows, dressing rooms, putting up with Mr. Richard's crowd.' And your brothers? They never complained. They always gave you anything you wanted."

Ursula continues, "And, you know what else, Lena? I have always been here to protect you, so it would never come to this. And in turn, all we've ever wanted is for you to make us proud, to see you dance on stage, like Ginger Rogers, always the finest act, the last act of the show."

Ursula makes a sweeping motion with her arm in the direction of the wall of pictures. "Look at these! Look at what you could have been." She sobs as she lowers her head into her hands, then is quiet. She stays in that pose for the longest time. Lena doesn't move a muscle.

Ursula gets a second wind—now raging. "And you ask me, 'What am I going to do, Mommy?' It certainly doesn't look like your teacher's going to marry you, does it? Well, young lady, you should have asked that before you let him have his way with you, huh? Where is he now? Where is he, Lena?"

Lena stares at the picture wall, teeth clenched, takes quick, shallow breaths as if she will cry.

"You've disgraced your family. And now, you don't have but two choices, and it appears that one has been eliminated. You've made your bed! You will go to a home for unweds, have that baby, and give it up for adoption. It should have been my own grandchild, but instead, it will be born out of wedlock, adopted out! A disgrace!"

Lena swallows, then ventures into the deep water, "Mr. Richard says he knows someone who can take care of it. He says that I don't have to go through with this."

Looking at her daughter, Ursula barks, "Take care of it? Take care of what?"

She pauses, her questions hanging in the air. "Are you talking about an abortion? A back-alley abortion? Girls die when they go to some quack to get rid of it. My cousin's girl, your second cousin, nearly died on someone's kitchen table trying to get rid of it. She got rid of it alright, but now she'll never have a baby. Is that what you want?"

Lena turned toward Ursula. "Linda? Almost died? You never told me that!"

"Of course I never told you that. That's not something you yak about when it's your own family."

Ursula continues, "I will not permit this. Having an abortion is against the law. So, if you don't die and you get caught, you go to jail. You ready for that?"

"But Mr. Richard says it's safe, Mom. He'll get Jerry to pay for it, and he'll go with me to get it done. Nobody will ever know."

"I'll know! You'd better call him. Your man of the hour. And tell him to get over here now. Right now! We've got some talking to do. Your father… oh my God. We've already lost one. Dear God!"

Just after dark, Ursula hears his car drive up and watches as Lena dashes past her, out the front door. He rejects her offer of an embrace, and she says something to him that Ursula can't hear as they both approach the front stoop. He looks toward the door with wrinkled eyebrows, nodding as they climb the porch stairs.

The three of them stand in the living room for an awkward moment, Lena reaching for Jerry's arm, him moving away just far enough to keep her from touching him. Ursula moves toward the kitchen table and motions them to sit. Before they sit, Jerry steps around to Ursula and, meeting her eyes, offers his hand, introducing himself, "Hello, Miss Ursula. I'm Jerry Spencer."

He offers a slight smile, and continues to meet her eyes, while holding out his hand.

Like he thinks I don't know who he is? Now embarrassed, Ursula takes his hand. She tries to look away, but his eyes hold her attention. Next, she attempts to extricate her hand, but he clasps her hand in both of his, shaking it lightly. She lets go again, but he holds fast and bends toward her. "I see where your daughter gets her beautiful eyes!"

She feels the blood rush to her face. He releases her hand and pulls a chair out for her, then helps her scoot her chair up to the table. She looks up at him and smiles. *He's such a gentleman. And so handsome!* She watches his face as he and Lena each take a seat at the kitchen table, he avoiding Lena's gaze.

Pushing aside the Avon sample bottles, Ursula tries to start the conversation, but only stammers. Lena says to

Jerry, "Mom knows about the baby and knows about Mr. Richard…"

He interrupts, "Let me just say, I understand why you are distressed—we all are—and I do want to help."

Ursula stares at Jerry, as though expecting him to continue. She finally finds her voice and speaks, "Well, Mr. Spencer. It seems you've already helped yourself to my daughter."

He meets her eyes. "I don't know how this happened, but I intend to be responsible. I certainly will pay for her procedure."

"You don't know how this happened, Mr. Spencer? I imagine it happened in the usual way, don't you think? Surely a history teacher can figure that out!"

She pauses, then realizing what he just said, she wrinkles her eyebrows and asks, "What procedure?"

"I'm here because I want to help Lena. Clearly, she's too young to have the baby, and quite young to be a wife, don't you think?"

Lena sniffs, her eyes glued to his face. He reaches over to pat her hand, but still avoids her gaze.

Ursula is impressed by his composure. She can see why Lena fell for him, but that changes nothing. *Unless he should want to marry her, of course.*

He continues, "I've only just met Mr. Richard, but he tells me Lena's life will be ruined if she has the baby, whether she gives it up or not, and he says she doesn't have to go through with having it. She's too young, he says. And talented. He says he knows a legitimate doctor. I can take care of the arrangements. But only if Lena agrees. She should be the one who decides. I can't be sure that it's mine, but I can certainly say that I will support her, whatever she wants to do."

Lena pulls away from Jerry, stands, her hands covering her stomach, "What do mean, you can't be sure? What do you mean? You know it's yours!"

He tries to touch her, but she recoils. With both hands, he motions for her to calm down. "I didn't mean anything, Lena. You say it's mine. That's all I know. I said I'd pay for the abortion, but I can't marry you—at least, not now. Can we sit down and talk?"

Ursula shoves her chair back and stands, arms crossed, looking at Lena, then at Mr. Spencer. "Are you saying I don't have a vote?"

Jerry jumps in before Lena can answer, "May your daughter and I have some time to talk? I have something to say about…"

Ursula interrupts, staring at him without blinking, "She is a minor, Mr. Spencer. A child, herself. And her options, as I see it, are for you to marry her and raise that baby together, or for her to have the baby and give it up for adoption. And there won't be any hiding this from your principal or from her father, no matter what happens now, Mr. Spencer. So you'd better figure out where you are in all this."

Ursula pauses briefly, then, even more emphatically, "And, Mr. Spencer, if Lena says it's yours, then it's yours."

He flinches visibly.

Ursula pivots to look at Lena, who finally asserts her independence. "Mr. Richard knows a doctor who can fix it so I don't have to have the baby."

"You mean abortion? We've already talked about that. I said no. Absolutely not!"

Moving closer to her mother, the two face off. "I'm not going to the unwed home to have this baby. I'm not going to have it at all. I'm sorry, Mother. Please say you'll help me. Please!

Ursula clutches Lena's shoulders as if she will shake her, but instead pulls her even closer. Now in her face, she says, "If you do this, you could die. God will punish you."

"How do you know? You don't even go to church!"

"That's enough, Lena."

Ursula lets go and Lena backs away.

"I'm going to go to Mr. Richard's house with Jerry so we can talk about this. It's my life, and I'm going to decide."

Jerry fidgets through this exchange, then Ursula walks into her bedroom and closes the door without another word to either of them.

She watches from her bedroom window as their taillights disappear, then collapses onto the edge of the bed and curls into a fetal position. She fills the empty house with her wails.

She wakes to the ringing. She shakes her head and quickly makes her way to the hallway to answer the telephone. "This is Jerry Spencer. May I talk with you for a minute?"

She nods her head, says nothing.

He speaks. "Hello? We, uh, Lena has an appointment after midnight with a doctor to determine what can be done. This doctor practices at the hospital, during the night. He's a real doctor, but that's all I can say about him. He could go to jail. And I can't say who told me about him. But Lena wants you to know. She wants to come home tomorrow. Is that alright?"

"None of this is alright. She's doing it tonight?"

"I don't know. It depends on the doctor. If she does, I'll bring her home when the doctor says it's safe, if that's okay."

There is a long silence, then Ursula speaks, "You should bring her home late afternoon tomorrow."

"Yes. Do you want me to call you after we see the doctor?"

"Are you staying with her?"

"Yes."

"Lena's dad will be here after midnight and I'm not going to tell him. So don't call me unless..."

Jerry reassures her, "I'm sure she'll be fine. I'm sorry about this. I'll try to make it up to Lena. Doing this'll be for the best, I think. Mr. Richard is very happy she is going to take care of this, and Lena is greatly relieved, I think."

Ursula continues, "Tell me the phone number there so I can call you first thing in the morning."

She writes his number on the pad next to the phone, and recites it back to him. She says again that she'll call him in the morning, then hangs up and goes into the kitchen to wait for Lena's father to get home from his second shift job at the G.E.

Ursula goes into the bathroom and looks into the mirror. She would swear that she has new lines on her face, on her forehead and especially around her eyes. She sits down on the stool and weeps into her hands for the loss of the child they'll never know, the loss of her daughter's innocence, and the grief they must hide from the world.

Jon doesn't need to know this. I don't know what would be worse—him knowing that she ended it, or knowing she had it and gave it away. Either way, it would destroy him. His little girl!

She makes her way back to the kitchen, takes the remains of the rhubarb pie she made yesterday from the Frigidaire, and sets it in the middle of the table. *He'll like this.* Then she puts the kettle on the stove to boil and takes two cups and two saucers from the cupboard. She opens the jar of Nescafé and spoons it into the cups, sets out the cream and sugar, and waits for the water to boil as she thinks about what will happen in some hospital room tonight.

A Good Heart

Goodman, the shop keeper, is in the front stocking shelves, and Dottie is in the back, grinding beef shoulders for hamburger when the call comes. He picks up the receiver and bellows into it with his usual cheerful salutation, "Goodman's Market here! If we ain't got it, you don't need it!"

Goodman smiles into the phone, and like always, speaks so his voice reverberates around the room. "Now, how can I help y…"

His cheerful greeting is interrupted by the impatient voice on the other end, asking if Dottie is there. He answers, "Well yes, she's here. Just a min…"

Interrupted again, he listens intently to the caller. An eruption from deep inside him spills into the room. He gains control, glances toward the back room, then quickly away and whispers, "Oh my God!" He's having trouble processing what he's hearing—Dottie's Vern has died. An accident at work. He's dead on the scene.

Dottie pushes the swinging door open with her shoulder and peeks around it, looking at him quizzically, "Everything okay?"

He says into the receiver, "Just a moment, please."

His hand over the mouthpiece, he turns to meet her gaze, composes himself enough to nod his head.

Dottie stands looking at him, her eyes still wrinkled, mouth poised as if to say something. Finally, she shrugs her shoulders and turns back to her work. The door swings shut behind her.

He picks up a pen, scrawls a number on the note pad by the phone, and speaks softly into the receiver. "Where is he now? Okay, I'll take care of it—we'll tell her and she'll call when she gets home."

Without replacing the receiver, he presses the lever to get a dial tone, and, turning away from the back room, he dials his home number.

When Helen answers, he speaks quickly, cupping his hand around his mouth to mute his voice. "We have a terrible problem, honey. Vernon has had an accident, or maybe a heart attack, they don't know yet…"

"Oh no! How awful! Dottie's Vernon? How is he doing?"

He pauses, looks at the floor. "Yes. Listen, honey. He died at the construction site where he was…"

Helen interrupts, "He died? Oh no! How awful for her. And for Rosie!"

"Yes, sweetheart. I know. It's terrible. Listen, Helen, can you call Gladys and ask her to come to the store right away? She's good friends with Dottie. It will help if she's here when I tell Dottie."

"Yes, I'll call her. I see her car, so she's home."

"Tell her what happened and ask if she can take Dottie home. I'll stay at the store until I can get someone to come in, then I'll help Dottie with whatever she needs."

"Sure, honey. What should we do with Rosie?"

"We'll have to get Dottie home first, then I'll get Rosie home later, when things settle down. Don't tell Rosie anything now, though. Okay? We've got to tell Dottie first."

He hangs up, and stands, frozen, looking out the store window. *How in the world can I tell her? What does one say? Your husband is dead? Or, I'm sorry to tell you that something bad has happened. You should call Vernon's foreman? And then what do I do when she starts bawling, or, worse, collapses? I just don't know…*

He does know he doesn't want a customer to be here when Dottie finds out, so he turns the open sign back to closed, pulls the shade down, then paces back and forth. *Dear God. Please get Gladys here soon!*

He knows how lucky he is to be married to Helen. *She'll know the right thing to do—where in the world would I be without her?*

In what seems like hours, but is really no time at all, Gladys pulls up and hurries into the store. He meets her at the door, and asks in a whisper while locking it behind her, "Did Helen tell you? You know what happened?"

She nods and looks around the store.

He whispers, "She's in the back room."

Just then, the door from the back room swings open. Dottie appears, grabs a towel to wipe her hands, and slides in behind the meat counter.

Smiling broadly, "Hi, Gladys. What can I get for you today? Having company over the weekend?"

Before Gladys can answer, Dottie looks over at her boss and instructs him, "Hey, don't you think you'd better open the shade and flip the sign? We're gonna be busy-busy-busy today!"

Gladys glances at Goodman and Dottie looks from one to the other. Neither of them is smiling, and neither is moving.

Dottie, confused, says, "Is everything okay?"

Gladys steps around the meat case to Dottie and takes her hand. "Dottie, I have some very bad news."

As if on cue, Goodman takes his place on her other side and as he tentatively puts his arm around her shoulders, she leans on him and pulls her hand away from Gladys. He gently guides her toward the "hubby" chair by the front door.

Dottie looks at him, and asks, almost inaudibly, "What's happened?"

He helps her to the chair to sit her down, but she resists, "What is it? What's happened?" She looks at Gladys, then repeats her question, "What's wrong? Tell me! Who is it?"

He steadies her and suggests that she sit, but Dottie, growing more and more agitated with each unanswered question, shrieks, "Is it Rosie? It's Rosie, isn't it?"

Goodman shakes his head, bends toward her and says, softly, "No, no, no, Dottie. It's not Rosie."

Gladys moves closer and speaks softly, "Rosie's fine, honey."

Dottie takes a deep breath, and looks from one to the other. She sinks into the chair and he stays by her with his hand on her shoulder. He nods to Gladys and she bends toward Dottie and says what he has not been able to say. "It's Vernon, Dottie. I'm afraid he's had an accident."

"An accident? At work? In the car? Where is he?"

As Dottie rises, unties her apron, she asks, "Is he in the hospital? Where…?"

"I'm afraid not, Dottie. I'm so sorry."

Gladys folds Dottie into her arms, and murmurs words of sympathy between sobs.

He stands, mute, looking on. *Neither of us has said it. Has said that Vernon died. That he's dead.*

Dottie looks at him, shakes her head, as though she is still not understanding what they are saying. When he sees her eyes begin to tear, he finally speaks, "I'm so sorry, Dottie. So sorry."

"Is he…?"

He moves toward the two women, nodding his head as the question reflects from Dottie's eyes. He reaches for her arm to steady her. "Yes, Dottie. A little over an hour ago. He passed, he died, before they could get him to the hospital. I'm so sorry…"

Her anguish penetrates the small shop as she collapses into his arms, the enormity of the message finally reaching all three of them.

They stand there, Goodman holding them both in an awkward embrace, while the women weep. As they break their hold and begin to verbalize their questions and confusion, he steps back, still holding Dottie's hand. "Dottie, Gladys is going to take you home now and she'll stay with you until your people get here. We'll both help you make the arrangements. And Dottie, you know you can count on me, on Helen and me, for anything you need. We'll bring Rosie over as soon as you're ready to have her home."

Dottie at first nods her head in agreement, then looking alarmed, says, "Does she know?"

Quietly, he answers, "No, Rosie doesn't know. That was Helen on the phone. Helen thinks Rosie should stay with her until you have some time to call your family and make arrangements for Vernon. Is that okay?"

"Where is he? Vern. Shouldn't I go? Stay with him? Where was he when…"

"He was at work, nailing up shingles on the house on Robinwood. He was on a ladder, they say, and suddenly he was on the ground, unconscious. The foreman says he never knew what hit him, Dottie. They aren't sure, but did he have a bad heart? They think it may have been a heart attack that made him fall. He's been working on ladders his whole life, so no one thinks he just fell."

Dottie covers her face and sobs into her hands. Goodman stands back and nods at Gladys as she again folds Dottie into her arms.

He feels so out of place, so unable to offer comfort. *I've never had to bury a family member of my own generation—I can't imagine having to…*

Again, Dottie asks him, "Where is he now?"

Goodman presses the note with a name and phone number written on it into her palm. "You can call his boss at this number when you get home. He was there when it happened. He knows what the authorities require when there's been a workplace injury, and he can answer your questions about what happened, Dottie. I'm sure he'll come over to the house as soon as you call him. He says that Vernon's body will be moved to Johnson's Funeral Home once they finish determining cause of…" He can't finish the sentence.

Dottie, staring straight ahead, finishes it for him. "Death."

Then, seemingly out of the blue, Dottie says, "I don't even know how to drive a car."

He and Gladys exchange a puzzled glance, then he helps Dottie up from the chair as he continues, "Gladys will drive you home now and she'll stay there with you. I'll be by when I get some help here, and I'll take you to Johnson's when you're ready to make the arrangements. Right now, I think you should go home and let Gladys help you call your people. Okay?"

He gently guides the two women out of the store and into Gladys's car, then stands in front of the shop watching, listening to the crunch of gravel as they drive away. He starts to wave, but thinks better of it.

Back inside, he leans on the closed door and stares in the direction of the butcher case, thinks about what will happen to Dottie now. His movements automatic, he raises the shade and turns the sign back to "open," then walks to the back room.

They're open early today, the day before Labor Day weekend. He knows that if this is like other holidays, everyone and their cousins will be coming in to pick up supplies for the end-of-summer picnics and the like. This is one of his five busiest days of the year.

His whole family, his wife Helen and all the kids big enough to work, they would all be here after breakfast to help out. Dottie's daughter, Rosie, is at the house helping Helen and is on call to entertain the little kids for most of the day.

His head is spinning with thoughts of Vernon—how someone can be alive one minute, and dead the next. *It could happen to anyone. He wasn't even old. It could happen to me, I guess, then where would Helen be?*

He picks up the phone to call his friend Lester from the lodge, asking if, by any chance, he'd be able to come in to cover the store this morning. When he explains the problem, Lester offers to bring his teenage son and his friend. They all know Dottie and they know the market routine as well. They'll be able to fill in as bag boys or whatever else is needed, he says.

They hang up, and the phone rings again—it's Helen wanting to make sure that he's found someone to help at the store. Also, she says that she has just talked to Reverend J.B. He will go to see Dottie a bit later this morning, and his wife is already on her way to the Goodman's home to watch the little ones so Helen can get to the store to help out. Helen says that Dottie wants Rosie to come home, so Gladys is on her way to pick up Rosie.

He's relieved to see that once people know, they change their plans on a dime and pitch right in to help. *The folks here—they're at their best when they're needed.* He's not sure that there's anywhere else on earth quite like Springdale. He's just thankful to live among such good people.

No sooner than he hung up with Helen than Lester's boys arrive. "Hi, Mr. Goodman. Dad dropped us off to start helping, and he says to say that he'll be back as soon as he drops Mom at the pharmacy. What would you like us to do first?"

Goodman smiles. "You boys hungry? If so, grab one of those Twinkies from the shelf and a bottle of pop from the cooler there. You can sit here at the card table and play Parcheesi or whatever—just you two relax until your dad gets here. You'll be helping him plenty. And I sure do appreciate you boys giving up your last Friday before school starts to help out!"

When Lester arrives, they chat a bit, and Goodman allows that Helen will be there shortly to operate the cash register and help with customer service.

While he's showing Lester how to sell meat from the case, someone comes into the store and walks up behind him. Before he turns to see who it is, he catches the scent of her perfume—feels her close to him. She touches his shoulder—her way of telling him that she's here now and that she'll take care of whatever needs doing. They always work so well together. It's a necessity with so many kids to raise and a business to run. He smiles, steps back and watches her for a moment, then realizes that, yes, she can handle this—in her sleep.

"I'm so glad you're here, sweetheart. I think I'll go on down to the funeral home and talk to Frank before I take

Dottie over there." He rambles on a bit, and Helen nods while organizing the cash register station. He continues, "This is so sudden for her. I mean, how is she going to manage? I can't even imagine having to… "

He paces in front of the door. "Are the kids okay? Ours, I mean? It was terrible. Telling her. Awful. I was so relieved that Gladys was here. And is Rosie…?"

Helen turns toward him and nods as he steps closer. They instinctively reach for each other, he wrapping her in a familiar, but unusually intense, embrace. His eyes squeeze shut, he feels a sob deep in his gut, but he holds it in.

He drifts, sounding somewhat confused, trying to share his thoughts. "I don't know why I feel so sad. It isn't that we, you know, we're not close, I mean Vernon and me? We never even… you know…" He pauses, then seeks her eyes, her assurance. "Maybe it's Dottie being so sad, not knowing what's next. Or maybe it's just… being here one minute and gone the next. How fast it happens. I don't know."

Helen, always wise, "It's okay, honey. It's normal to feel this way. It's shocking, actually. And Dottie's a friend, so we feel for her."

She walks him toward the door. "You go on ahead. Dottie will appreciate your help with the funeral arrangements. And the fresh air will do you good."

He's absorbed in thought as he walks the eight blocks, in a deliberate rhythm, to Johnson's Funeral Home, trying to work through what he's feeling about Vernon's passing.

For one, I never really knew Vernon. But Dottie's such a nice lady. Him? He was never in my circle of friends. Not a Mason. Didn't even go to church.

Then, as Helen often mused about him, he began mumbling to himself, "Well, heck. Most I ever saw him was when he'd pick up Dottie, in his truck, her with a bag of groceries. If the truth were known, I never saw him help her at all."

Then, right out loud, *"Is he even worth all this grief? I guess everybody gets a send-off, even if they're worthless. And who am I to judge?"*

He turns his thoughts to Dottie. *She's going to need a real job, full-time, to take care of Rosie. She's going to need our help until she gets back on her feet.*

He looks up and sees the sign on the new supermarket and says, out loud, "I'm not even sure the shop will survive Goll-dern Kroger's!"

He surprises himself when he hears himself almost swearing about the new supermarket. He knows this weekend is going to be a test of the competition, and he can see their parking lot from here—already more cars than he's seen there any time of day. Right now, he's not in the mood to get closer to Kroger's than this, so he turns right and heads down the block toward the back of the funeral home, and his thoughts turn back to Vernon.

Well, heck. No matter what, I can't help but believe Dottie'll be better off down the road. What with his drinking and all. Truth is, no one seemed to like him all that much. That time he came to the Good Friday service at church drunk as a skunk, cryin' about whatever, and they had to escort him out? That was awful. Interrupted the reverend while he was preaching! Embarrassed Dottie to death. Poor thing!

Approaching the funeral home, he sees Frank Johnson in his open garage, wheeling a casket around and sliding it into his new hearse—a Cadillac, at that.

He knows Frank, not well, but so-so—darn near impossible to not know the funeral director in a town this size. His people don't go to Goodman's church. They go to the Baptist church on the other side of town. All the Goodmans are Methodist. Always have been.

I've never seen Frank when he wasn't well turned out—dressed to the nines! And his hair! It's all glossy. Must be Brylcreem. I hear it attracts the ladies, but I swear, I've never seen him with a woman.

Goodman walks over to greet him. "Hello, Frank. Mighty fine wagon you've got there. That a '52?"

"Sure is. Brand new. We like to treat our customers very well, like royalty, you know?"

I imagine you do.

He wonders how in the world Dottie is going to pay for being treated like royalty. He hears it's gotten so expensive to bury a loved one. That it can cost well over a thousand bucks. That even life insurance isn't enough to pay for it. He heard that the Smiths are still sending Frank payments every month for burying their mother more than a year ago.

Frank speaks up, obviously understanding why Goodman is there. "We're going to the morgue to pick up Vernon just as soon as I get the call. His wife at home now?"

Goodman nods. *It's odd that he still calls him Vernon. Not Vernon's body or the corpse, or...*

"You wanna come in and sit a spell, Goodman?"

"Sure thing, Frank."

They enter the funeral home from the side door to the private quarters rather than the public door. The parlor always smells sickeningly sweet to Goodman, like the scent you get when you spray from one of those aerosol cans with a picture of flowers on it, the kind people spray in their bathrooms. He's relieved that it's not so funeral smelling here in the private area.

He thinks for a minute, crosses his arms, and says to Johnson. "Look here, Frank. I'm worried about Dottie—she's likely still in shock. You know what I mean? She doesn't have anyone here—they all live either in Arkansas or Detroit, and I imagine they won't be here for another day or so, if at all. I don't expect that she has any extra money lying around either, and I'd be real surprised if she even has a policy on him. So, I'll bring her here when she's ready to come and I'll stay with her, help her understand everything. That all right with you?"

"Sure, of course. Probably won't get him until later this afternoon anyway. They may do an autopsy—it's required sometimes. If it's an accidental death, you know? May be important for Dottie to know. We can make arrangements any time."

"I'm talking about her understanding what you'll try to sell her. Sometimes looks like you guys are pressuring folks to spend more than they have. Now, I know you'd like to sell her the finest casket and all the services, the whole shebang. That's how you make your living. I know that."

"Then what are you gettin' at?"

"I'm saying that she doesn't need more grief than she already has. She doesn't have anyone to help her decide, or to help her pay for all this, and your pressure may just be more than she can handle. You understand?"

"Sure, yes. I understand."

"So, let's talk about what you're going to recommend to Dottie when I bring her in. Just so I understand?"

"Sure. We have a range of services and quality in caskets, including burial vault, embalming, of course, visitation and funeral. The price really depends on the items and services she chooses, like in your store. You know? But we'll do right by her."

Just then, the phone rings. Frank speaks curtly to whomever is on the other end, and when he hangs up, he says, "Gotta go, Goodman. Gonna go pick him up now. I'll call her when we get him in."

He holds the door open and motions to Goodman, "Come on. I'll drop you at your car. Give you a ride in my new Caddy."

When Goodman arrives at Dottie's house, he sees several cars and knows that neighbors and friends will be there to help out. Once inside, he doesn't see Dottie, but he spots Ursula from down the street, bustling around the dining area. Already on the table are two casseroles, a platter of cookies, and a huge bouquet of mixed flowers. He smells something cooking and hears the voices of other women in the kitchen.

Gladys speaks first. "Well, hello! Come on in. Dottie's lying down until the funeral home calls. You know Ursula, don't you?"

He nods, smiles.

"Oh well, of course. You know everyone in this town!" Gladys chirps.

He greets Ursula. "Looks like you have things under control? Listen, if you need anything at all, you go on ahead and call Helen. She's at the store with Lester, and he'll get in his truck and bring whatever you need."

He asks Gladys, "How's she doing?"

"Oh, what do they say? She's doing as well as can be expected."

"Was she able to get ahold of her family? How many you suppose will be coming?"

"I think there's two carloads coming up from Arkansas—they're his people—and some of her folks will be in from Detroit and Missouri—all either in the middle of the night or tomorrow morning."

"Okay. We'll need to find some beds for them. Shouldn't be a problem. Helen will call some folks."

Out of the corner of his eye, he spots Rosie sitting by herself on the back stoop, so he eases out the back door, sits down next to her.

"Hi, Rosie, you okay?"

"Yes, sir."

He hears a wobble in her voice, wishes he knew how to comfort her. They sit, neither speaking, listening to the chatter coming from the kitchen. One voice, more distinct than the others, can be heard above the chatter. "She didn't even cry when her mother told her!" And then another voice adds, "Shows you something. She's adopted, you know."

He was sure that Rosie heard it, too. She looks at him, her eyes searching for an answer to a question she hadn't asked.

He stands and offers his hand. "Why don't we take a short walk? I need to go by the church and see when the reverend is coming over."

She nods. He takes her hand, and they walk through the grass to the street, neither uttering a sound.

Once on the street, they make their way toward the park and the church just beyond. He puts his arm around her shoulders and she inches closer to him, then lengthens her stride so they can walk in unison.

"So, your Mom told you what's happened?"

Rosie nods, looks down. "She told me he died, but they don't know why."

"Listen, Rosie. What those women said? That's just gossip. Everyone is different. Some people cry all the time, and some never do. You're allowed to be Rosie, to feel exactly the way you feel."

She nods, says nothing. He doesn't know exactly how to draw her out, so he gets right to the point. "You seem worried, Rosie. Would you like to talk about it?"

He sees her head nod, but hears only their footsteps.

She finally speaks, "My mom says she doesn't know what she's going to do. How she's going to manage without…"

She pauses, her voice wobbly. He allows the long silence so she can finish her thought.

She continues, "What, uh… what… will happen…? I mean, do I have to go back?"

He stops and turns toward her. "Back where, Rosie?"

When he looks into her eyes, he sees fear.

Fighting back tears, she sobs, "Where I was, the home. What if she doesn't have enough money to keep me? My real mom couldn't keep me either."

He is stunned. "Oh, dear girl! No, no, no—you're not going anywhere. When your mom, Dottie, adopted you, she became your real mom. Your Forever Mom. And she needs you now like you needed her then. Understand what I'm saying?"

Rosie nods, sniffling, wiping her runny nose on the inside of her sleeve.

As they continue toward the church, he glances her way. "Rosie, you're old enough to help out, help take care of things. Like you do for the kids and for Helen, right? You're how old?"

"Fourteen. Almost."

"Right. We just have to help your mom through this, one day... what do we say?"

She chimes in with him, "One day at a time." She looks at him and her lips part in a slight smile.

"C'mon. Let's go talk to the reverend and then I'm going to take your mom down to Johnson's to make arrangements. You can stay and help out in the kitchen or just help Miss Gladys with whatever she needs."

Rosie seems satisfied, and Goodman is glad he took the time to talk to her. He feels sad for Rosie. She's been part of Dottie's family for—how long's it been?—four or five years? He doesn't even think of her as an adopted child. *Imagine! She's worried about being sent back to wherever she lived before! Who would do that?*

They continue walking, both quiet.

She's always so sweet to the kids. The little ones love her to death! Even little Maryann—whenever Rosie is at the house, Maryann won't let anyone else touch her!

They arrive at the parsonage and Goodman rings the bell. The reverend, who they can see through the screen door, is on the phone, and he motions for them to come in. Goodman holds the door open for Rosie and they go inside, wait nervously in the vestibule.

When he's finished with his call, Reverend J.B. motions them in. "You're here about Vernon?" He turns to Rosie, who is studying all the knickknacks on the book shelf next to her, and asks, "How are you, little lady?" She nods.

Goodman offers his hand. "Hello, Reverend. Just stopped in to see what time you expect to come by to see Dottie. I'm going to take her over to Johnson's to make arrangements, and can do that now, or wait until you've seen her. I talked with him earlier and he said we'd probably want to do the funeral on Sunday afternoon because, of course, Monday's the holiday. I think Dottie'll want to have the service at the parlor."

The reverend nods and adds, "Sure then. Give me a call when you get back home from Johnson's, will you? I'll work with Dottie to schedule it, if she wants me to handle it. And I assume she will. And yes, at Johnson's rather than the church. He wasn't a member or even a believer, far as I know. We'll sure take care of Dottie—she is a dear person and, as you know, a long-time member."

Rosie watches the two men's exchange. Goodman signals to her that they are leaving, and he guides her down the porch steps.

When they arrive back at the house, he waits by the door and asks Rosie, "Will you go in now and tell your mom I'm here to take her to Johnson's?"

Dottie and Goodman arrive at Johnson's Funeral Home—this time through the front, public door—stepping through the reception area into the now empty parlor where Vernon's body will be displayed. Everyone in town has been in this room at one time or another, Dottie included, but she looks around as though she's never seen it before. She says to Goodman that it feels strange—she's never been here when it was empty and brightly lit. As she looks around, he sees that her face is expressionless—there are no tears, though her eyes, swollen and puffy, convey her sorrow.

Frank, now wearing a suit the color of butterscotch with a burgundy shirt and a stylish tie, greets them using her formal name, Mrs. Wright, even though Goodman thinks Frank knows her well enough to call her Dottie. His voice and manner are syrupy and overly solicitous as he escorts her away from Goodman, making it clear that he wants to address her, rather than them. Goodman is close enough to hear him speak about his compassionate assistance regarding her selection of funeral and burial services, and hears him wax on about Vernon's deep roots in the community. But when he talks about his commitment to helping Dottie create a highly personal funeral and burial service, one that truly reflects the dignity of the life that Vernon lived, who he was to his community and how he will be remembered, Goodman turns away, holds a clenched fist to his mouth to stifle the remark he might have made.

Frank asks Goodman to take a seat while he shows Dottie the burial vessels downstairs, but Dottie says, politely, that she'd like him to accompany them. No explanation.

Frank takes Dottie's elbow and leads her to the elevator with Goodman following close behind. The elevator down opens to a large showroom, one that Goodman has not seen before. Rather than the basement he expected, the room was decorated with silky wall paper and plush carpeting. It is a showcase for a dozen or more coffins, or "caskets," as Johnson calls them, all open and lit from special fixtures on the ceiling.

Frank is talking to Dottie in that same cloying tone, and Goodman sees that he's in a full-court press, determined to make a high dollar sale. "As you can see, Mrs. Wright, most of these caskets are half-couch (the top half opens) but a few are full-couch, all have satin interior linings, some quilted and some with designs. All have hermetical seals, of course. Each of these beautiful caskets will make a statement about your family's regard for the deceased."

And then pointing to each, he further describes the outside. "Starting in this row, you have your solid woods, carved so beautifully, aren't they? Oak, mahogany, walnut, even maple. Then you have your solid bronze, stainless steel, and, of course, the plain eighteen-gauge steels in different colors. They're off in the back there."

Dottie finally speaks, her voice shaking, "Well, I'd like to see the prices before we look at these coffins here.

Can I see that first? I mean, how much will all this cost? Do you have anything simpler?"

Goodman, feeling Dottie's distress, discreetly moves to her side while Frank continues his pitch, "Sure enough, Mrs. Wright. These are the caskets that come with our funeral packages. We have several. Packages, that is, depending on the casket you choose, of course. We do have the plywood coffins covered with cloth, different colors and some patterns, but we don't display those on the floor here because most people want their loved ones to be shown and buried in a more beautiful and, of course, durable casket. The plain wood coffins are usually used for pauper cremations, whereas, of course, most of our people bury their loved ones at the cemetery. Do you have a plot for him, or will we need to purchase that for you? Or will this be a cremation?"

Goodman finally adds his two cents, "Look here, Frank. This poor woman has been through the wringer today. Can we just see the price of all of this so she can get home to her family?"

Frank responds as though he's been scolded, "This is exactly why, Goodman, we advise folks to make these arrangements in advance, so they don't have to make these choices under stress."

Back in Frank's office, he pulls out a contract, puts it on a clip board, and says to Dottie, "I'm assuming you have a policy on him, right? Most people have a thousand. We handle that—part of our service to you. We'll get his notarized death certificate and submit all the paperwork so you won't have to worry at all. Send an obit to the Gazette. We'll do all of it for you."

Dottie looks down, then gives a sidelong glance at Goodman, and without her saying anything, he can see that Vernon has no insurance policy. He frowns at Frank.

Frank, oblivious to this signal, continues, "All of our packages include embalming, casket and burial vault, transport to and from our facility, the wake, and burial. The plot is extra, adding another, say, $200. We can arrange for that if you like. Most people have a plot in the family already."

He continues, "We'll be able to do this for you, Mrs. Wright, for under $2000. That includes the beautiful oak casket with everything except the plot. $1999. It's a really good price."

Goodman hears Dottie gasp. He reaches over, lays his hand on hers.

Frank, seeing Dottie's reluctance, retrenches, "We can go down in quality, the casket, if that's what you want. The eighteen-gauge steel boxes for less money don't have a hermetical seal. We can't guarantee that it won't come open later, underground, you know? But there are some in-between, of course."

Goodman is watching Dottie, hoping that she can hold it together until they finish here. She asks if she can go to the restroom and Frank points her in the direction.

While she's gone, Goodman takes advantage of being alone with Frank. "How much does the embalming cost, Frank?"

"The embalming? You don't want to skip that, Goodman. He won't make it to Sunday."

Goodman continues, "What if the casket stays closed? No one wants to look at old dead Vernon. She doesn't have insurance, Frank. And this is more money than she takes home in a whole year. And what about the vault? What does that add? Give me a price for just the steel casket, no embalming, and no vault. Closed casket."

"Okay. I can take it down to $849—that's with no embalming, the eighteen-gauge steel casket, and no vault. Out of here on Sunday."

Dottie comes back into the office. Johnson continues, "Okay, Dottie. I can make it $849. That's the eighteen-gauge steel casket, no vault, no seal, and without embalming, which is what Goodman here thinks you should do. That'll mean we have a closed casket event. Are you okay with that?"

Dottie looks at Goodman, who nods his head, and she looks back at Frank and nods her head.

Frank continues, "If you want to see him before we close it up, you should come an hour before we have public viewing, or rather public visiting. First thing tomorrow morning. Will that work for you?"

In a very subdued tone, she asks, "Do you have a payment schedule? I'm not sure…"

Johnson excuses himself to find another contract for her to sign, and she stares after him, then shifts her eyes to Goodman. "I don't know. I'm afraid Vern's family will be upset that he doesn't have a nice coffin and that they won't get to see him. I mean, most people are seen lying in their coffins, aren't they? They never look like themselves though, do they? But will they—his family—think I'm disrespecting him? With a cheap coffin, I mean, and no embalming?"

Goodman doesn't think her questions need answering as much as she needs reassurance that she's doing the right thing, so he tries to help. "You are being sensible and that does not mean disrespectful, Dottie. If you spend as much on this funeral as Johnson would like, you'll be taking the food out of Rosie's mouth—and putting it in Johnson's bank account! Think of it that way."

"But, will no embalming make him rot and let things get in his coffin? With no seal on it? Or vault? I mean worms and such?"

"Dottie, if Vernon's brothers and sisters want him embalmed and want a Cadillac coffin, maybe they should chip in some cash! Meanwhile, Vernon won't know what coffin he's in or why. You realize this, right?"

He found himself getting a little huffy, and though he didn't want to come across as uncaring about Vernon's family, he was aggravated that, on top of everything she has to worry about, Dottie should have to be concerned about them approving of his funeral. Furthermore, he is aggravated that Johnson pretends to care so darn much about the dead person's dignity or whatever, but cares so little about Dottie. She's the one left alone, without even an insurance policy to tide her over. Good grief!

Frank returns with a blank contract, and a list of packages and what they include, and Goodman tells him that he'll look it over and bring it by later on.

Dottie and Goodman leave the funeral home in silence. As he helps her into the car, Frank steps outside and gives him a signal that he has something else to say. Goodman shuts the car door and walks over to him.

Frank, making sure Dottie is out of earshot, has another offer. "There is another way we can save money, Goodman. We can embalm him and show him in the nice oak casket, then move him to a simple plywood coffin just before the burial. We drape it and lower it into the grave so that people can't really tell it's a different box. No one will ever even know it. And we all win because Vernon is shown in a nice box, and we look respectable. No vault, of course, and no seal."

Goodman listens to Johnson, but can't quite believe that he's hearing this. "Is that even legal, Frank? How much do we even save with that scheme?"

"I can do it for $549. So she'd save $300, that's on the cost of the casket itself. I'll throw in the embalming. No cemetery plot, though. She needs to buy that separately."

Goodman, still in disbelief, walks back to the car and drives Dottie home.

Later that afternoon, Goodman pulls up in the driveway in front of the funeral home. Frank comes out to meet him, and they talk through the open window of his car.

Goodman holds the contract in his hand and tells Frank, "I have here a contract for the steel, she wants grey, open casket funeral with embalming for $500, and, in my hand, a check for an additional $249, call it the down payment. $749 total." He hands the document and the check to Frank.

Frank congratulates Goodman on their choosing a much more dignified funeral. "But that would be the $849, not the $749 option."

Goodman holds up his hand, "Wait just a minute Frank. I'm handing you a check for $249 right now, and I will loan Dottie the $500 on the contract, so you'll get all your money up front rather than having to wait years to get it back, if you even do. For that, I'm taking the $100 discount. Like you said, you can throw in the embalming. And you won't have to do any finagling of a corpse from one box to another, trying to make people think they're getting something they're not." Frank stares at the contract, says nothing.

"One more thing, Frank. Don't mention this arrangement to Dottie or any other soul. I told her that you agreed to $500, and I want to keep it that way. I'm doing this for my own reasons that have nothing to do with you."

"Take it or leave it Frank." He rolls up his window and drives away.

On his way back to the store, he passes by the Kroger supermarket, and sees that their lot is still nearly full. He notes that Kroger was able to pave their parking lot, whereas his is gravel. It doesn't matter too much, but it says something about a place when they have enough money to pave the lot.

He hasn't told anyone except Helen that he's had talks with some real estate men downtown. One of his Masonic friends put them in touch because folks know he's worried that the new supermarket will drive him out of business. The real estate guys would like to expand to Springdale and have offered him a job selling commercial real estate right here in his home town. He'd be perfect, they say, because he knows just about everyone in town, and everyone trusts him. And they've made a real good offer—he feels he could support his family on that and then some. It's way more money than he makes now. They don't know that. But it is. He hasn't decided yet, but he's relieved that there is a way forward for him and his family.

He does agree that his butcher shop isn't going to be able to compete with the supermarket for groceries, but he hopes that if he keeps the shop, it can clear enough with just meat and poultry sales to support Dottie and a butcher. He could manage the back, and Dottie can take care of the front of the store.

Now, what with Vernon dying and all, he may need to make the move sooner than later. That's if Dottie wants to come back. Even if he goes to work selling real estate, he can oversee the purchasing and accounts at the store, and turn just the operations over to her. Whenever she gets back to work.

It's hard for him to imagine not being at the shop every day, not seeing the town folk (mostly the women) who come in, day after day, sharing stories about their kids, exchanging recipes. Some of the older men too, sitting at the card table playing Parcheesi, passing the time of day.

But now, with Dottie's needing to be the bread-winner, it may push him toward making the change. He knows it's just a matter of time.

They say when the Lord closes a door, he opens a window. We'll just have to see.

Back at the store just after closing time, the two Goodmans are alone again, talking about the events of the day. Helen, who's counting the money and adding receipts, tells him that business was quite slow today, unlike past Labor Days. She blames Kroger and he agrees. He tells her when he walked up that way early this morning, just after Dottie and Gladys left, that there were more cars in their lot than he could count on both hands. And that just now, the parking lot is still full.

He watches her as she organizes the receipts, holding paper clips between her lips, totally engrossed in what she's doing. He remembers when they first met, how beautiful she was—turquoise ribbons that helped contain her auburn curls. For them, date night was an evening at the roller rink where all the boys tried to get a turn around the floor with her. He can't remember now when they last went to the rink. Before they were even married, he thinks. Since then, all the babies have taken a toll on her figure, but to him, she's more beautiful than ever.

They sit at the card table talking about their day and he tells her what they've always thought—that Frank has a sleazy operation going on there. "First," he tells her, "every absolute thing is way overpriced—the caskets, the burial, embalming, the transport—everything." He launches into a rant. "Johnson starts—STARTS!—at $2000, and that doesn't include the plot, for Pete's sake!"

She looks up. "Really? Two thousand dollars?"

"Yes! And second, Frank is re-using caskets."

"What? What do you mean, re-using caskets?"

"He uses a fancy casket for showing, then switches the body to a crummy plywood box for burying. He drapes it in a fancy cloth so no one can tell. Who knows what else he's chintzing on!"

She looks horrified at the thought. "Does Dottie even know about that?"

"No. And I'm not going to tell her, either."

He goes on. "I got him down to $749, but it wasn't easy. And, sweetheart, I should have asked you in advance, but I thought you'd be fine with our helping her out, so I… we paid Frank directly $249. Dottie doesn't know about that part."

He finishes his confession. "And we loaned her the rest, $500. I felt I had to do that. She's been so loyal to me, us really. She and Rosie. I don't even really care if she pays it back, but I know she will do her best."

Helen, of course, approves with her classic smile and a simple nod of her head. "That's all fine, of course, sweetheart. You're a wonderful friend."

He goes on. "And I know things may get tight for us, with the shop not doing so well, but I imagine I'll be starting the new job sooner than I thought. As soon as Dottie is ready to come back to work, we'll start making some changes."

Because of Helen's inheritance, they've never had the kind of money troubles that so many of their friends in the community have. They both realize that they are fortunate to be able to help folks in a time of need, but they're adamant about keeping it anonymous or at least private.

Even so—the town folk?—they all know who the anonymous donor is.

Helen finishes putting away the cash register receipts and walks over to him, reaches for his hands, pulls him up, and looks into his eyes. "I love you so for your generosity, Goodman."

They hug, and he repeats what he's said so often. "I don't help folks for the recognition. My reason is purely selfish. It makes me feel good to be the messenger who brings gifts to those in need. And besides, I believe your father would approve of how we have carried on his spirit of generosity. That, and your love, Mrs. Goodman—that's enough for me.

He smiles and says in his impish way, "Hey, honey. You wanna' go skating tonight?"

They both chuckle, then walk hand-in-hand across the gravel lot to their car. As they head toward home, he takes a turn and drives really slow by Kroger's.

"Look at that, Helen. They're still open—right through the dinner hour. And look at all the customers they have!"

She looks straight ahead. "Tsk, tsk, tsk. Anymore, I don't know what's becoming of this world."

Acknowledgements

This project would never have gotten off the ground were it not for the patience, encouragement and positive but honest feedback from my fellow writers and dear, dear friends, Elizabeth G. and Judy K. We gather when possible, on Wednesday mornings at Beans & Bagels in Frederick for what has become an almost sacred ritual—coffee, bagels and critiques. Owners Rich and Lisa, and their staff at B&B always have a friendly greeting and give us all the time we need at the back table.

To my friends and fellow writers who answered my calls after the stories were told—most especially Elizabeth G. who did the hard work of proof editing—thanks for taking the time to read, again (and again). And many thanks to Mary C. who, for the first time, ventured into unknown waters to read, give to me nuanced feedback and encouragement.

In this blossoming self-publishing industry, there are people stepping up right and left to provide assistance to authors who have finished the writing and are now ready to share their stories in the marketplace of books. Thanks to Kira T. at MaiaSocial.com who expertly proofed the formatted manuscript and helped to bridge the gap between the art form and the technology needed to get it into print and into the hands of the readers.

Most special thanks to Beth C. at Write Directions—the writers' cheerleader, coach and go-to person for great advice and all things writing/publishing/launching. Her encouragement and advice proved to be the fuel that took me over the finish line.

I can't say enough about the talented Argentinian graphics designer, Agustina G. (ours is an online relationship), who designed the book cover and SailAway logo. It was a delight working with her across two continents and several languages. Her response to the minutiae of cover design changes was instantaneous and done with a smile I could feel across the miles.

And, of course, deep gratitude goes to John, who not only encourages me to continue writing, but always reads and sometimes even critiques my manuscripts.

Finally, I thank Samantha, who always reminds me that it's time for a puppy cookie and a few laps up and down the stairs.

About the Author

Judith lives with her husband, John, and curly Cavachon, Samantha, in Frederick, MD. They are also Nana and Papa to three darling grands who live close by with their parents.

During her ten years of sailing on their schooner, Thaleia, many of her articles and essays on a wide variety of topics were published in various sailing magazines, journals and newspapers, both in the U.S. and in the Caribbean. Currently, when she's not writing, she spends time helping local theatre non-profits in Frederick, and is a tireless advocate for and supporter of the performing arts.

Made in the USA
Middletown, DE
18 May 2019